OUT OF THE DARK

CŌNFINGŌ PUBLISHING

OUT OF THE DARK

DAVID GAFFNEY

First published in the UK in 2022 by Confingo Publishing

249 Burton Road, Didsbury, Manchester M20 2WA

www.confingopublishing.uk

Cover photograph by Zoë McLean
Typesetting by John Oakey
Printed by TJ Books Limited

A CIP catalogue record for this book is available from the British Library

ISBN 978-1-7399614-0-4

2 4 6 8 10 9 7 5 3 1

For Clare

PART ONE

PART ONE

CHAPTER ONE

1988

A name badge dangled from around the housing officer's neck but I didn't bother to read it and I don't think he expected me to. He leaned his elbow on the reception desk and rested his chin in his hand.

'How are you today?' he said in a soft voice, as if I was fragile and he didn't want to disturb my equilibrium.

'I'm OK,' I said. 'How are you?'

'Well, there's no sign of those extra-terrestrials yet.' He glanced up at the ceiling. 'The ones who were going to come down and save us all.'

'No,' I said. 'It's all hollow promises with that lot, isn't it?'

'You are so right. Well – how can we help you today?'

'I'm interested in 69 Acacia Avenue on the Yew Tree Estate.'

'Oh,' he said, his voice becoming louder and reaching an almost normal level. 'You're the second person to ask about that flat.' He stood up straight. 'Isn't that where the old black and white film was made?'

'That's what they say.'

'The last enquirer about 69 Acacia was a female person.

Very glamorous, or must have been at one time, if you know what I mean.'

This news surprised me. But who knows. Another film enthusiast like me? An extra from a crowd scene?

A rapid succession of loud bangs came from the back office and made us jump.

'Fizzy wine,' the housing officer said. 'Somebody leaving or somebody's birthday. There's always something going on round here.'

He leaned his arm on the counter once more and spoke quietly to me again, as if conspiring.

'She said she had filmed something in that flat. A scene. And could she get inside to have a look round.'

He raised his eyebrows at me as if I might know what all this was insinuating.

'I want to rent it for a short time,' I said.

He stood up straight again.

'I told her that she'd have to wait until there was a tenant in there and she could ask them.'

'So it's empty?'

'Let me have a look.'

He went over to a hook-board full of keys with handwritten labels under each one.

'You're in luck,' he said, lifting up the keys with a jaunty motion then tossing them in the air and catching them in his other hand. 'Moved out last week. You can't have it permanent, though. Short term, as you're not on our housing list. Nor are you' – he looked me up and down – 'a member of one of our priority groups. There's just a little bit of paperwork,' he said, bringing a large file out from under the desk.

More corks popped in the office at the back and there were cheers, whoops and some handclaps.

The flat was on the seventh floor of a seven-storey block, one of an identical pair that stood at an angle to each other next to the intersection of the M5 and M6 motorways, just between West Bromwich and Walsall. I liked the incongruous address – Acacia Avenue, the Yew Tree Estate: a block named after an African shrub, on a council estate named after trees found in English graveyards.

It turned out that no one wanted to live in these flats. They were far away from everything, and some considered the area dangerous, always mentioning the big empty area of grass and the fact that teenaged kids congregated on it at night. I had a special reason for renting this particular flat. It was rumoured that it had been used as a location for *Out of the Dark*, a film I had studied at the nearby Walsall Institute of Higher Education under the tutorage of Dr Ian Colley. *Out of the Dark* was a key movie in the film noir strand, and after this course, film noir became my obsession. In my opinion, *Out of the Dark* was one of the most perfect examples of the genre, and all the more fascinating because while most of the classics of the film noir canon had been made in the forties on B-movie sets in Los Angeles, *Out of the Dark* was made in the sixties, in England, here in the West Midlands, with most of its action taking place in Birmingham city centre.

The film had all of the usual themes and tropes of film noir: the dreamy half-real worlds, the shadows, the sex, the death, the Freudian suppression of desire, the transgression, the femme fatale, everything. It was little known outside of film studies courses and nerdy cine magazines and, partly owing to its obscurity and cult status, I had become a kind

11

of unofficial expert on it. I had written an article about it for *Sight & Sound* and had been interviewed for a documentary on Radio 4. I had become the film's official historian and was a strong advocate for the work whenever it came up for discussion in the media. If you wanted a comment about *Out of the Dark*, you came to me, Daniel Quinn; the way in later years you went to Mark Kermode for quotes about *The Exorcist*.

And here I was. In the flat, the actual flat, where it was rumoured that one or more of the scenes involving Eva Ni Riain, played impeccably by the gorgeous Mathilde Pelletier, were filmed.

The flat was almost empty – just a sofa, a high wooden stool like you'd have at a breakfast bar, and a grey plastic stacking chair. It smelt of paint and damp and tobacco and in some weird, homeopathic way, I felt I could sense that someone had been crying in the flat recently, as if this sadness had seeped into the walls. These walls were covered in circular patches of dark mould, where the ends of the metal girders were positioned. The man at the housing office had warned me about this, and told me it was condensation damp, caused by the previous tenants drying their clothes inside.

The first thing I did was set up the VHS player and the television so I could quickly get to work on watching the film. Then I slid the videotape out from its cardboard case and pushed it into the machine. I enjoyed every element of this old movie. So much so, I would sometimes watch a single scene in the slowest of slow motion, or sit before a series of frozen sections frame by frame, like a procession of static paintings. This habit could be useful now, because to find what I was looking for (and I didn't know exactly what I needed to find, but I had a rough idea) I might have to resort to that method.

I had tried to watch the film at my parents' house in Cumbria; I had the tape with me, but I couldn't concentrate on it. They would come into the room while I was watching and start up a conversation about something mundane, as if they were in a sixth-form play. I knew they were all wondering how I could sit and watch an old film when I had gone through such a traumatic time. So I couldn't stay there in Cumbria to watch it. I just couldn't. The way people looked at me all the time. With a kind of, I was going to say pity, but it wasn't pity, it was something different, more like an excess of care. I didn't want to be looked at like that all the time, with that cloying softness in their eyes. I could feel myself being twisted into a certain shape, a shape that they could easily fit around. So I wanted to be in a different place where I could learn how to be myself again. Learn how to become a new me in these new circumstances. And to do that I needed to find out who the new me was. That's why I took my precious VHS cassette and boarded a train to Birmingham.

Tonight I would watch the film in its entirety without taking any notes at all. Try to experience it as a piece of entertainment the way an ordinary viewer would. Maybe what I was looking for would slip into the front of my mind when I wasn't concentrating. Maybe that's what would happen.

'Untamed desire leads to murder in this tangled film noir set in a gritty northern English town.' That's how the *Time Out Film Guide* describes *Out of the Dark* (1962). But that description doesn't do justice to the complexities of the plot, nor explain why this film made such an important contribution to the tiny canon of British noir.

Directed in Birmingham by Otto Schneider, a former lighting cameraman for Fritz Lang, the movie has a German Expressionist aesthetic and a modernist, edgy feel. Its portrayal of uneasy industrial relations in a dysfunctional car manufacturing plant makes it an important landmark in social history. However, what stays with the viewer is the picture it paints of the city's lawless underbelly, as well as a powerful sense that a new transgressive sexuality has been unloosed and is prowling our country unsupervised and out of control. The music is by the Polish composer Krzysztof Penderecki, whose work was used later in *The Exorcist* and *The Shining*. At that time it was usual for a European crime movie to have a bawdy jazz soundtrack, so this contemporary score for full orchestra marked *Out of the Dark* as something very different. The score – atonal, dissonant, and at times terrifying – makes the experience like a hideous dream you want to quickly forget. Or, as film critic Clive James put it: 'Nasty people doing nasty things to each other in nasty places somewhere in the north of England, mostly in the dark, and usually while it's raining.' It's not the north of England, it's the West Midlands, but I had to admit the rest of the quote is fairly accurate.

As I said, the actress who played femme fatale Eva Ni Riain was called Mathilde Pelletier. Half French, half Indian, Pelletier had a curious way of stopping mid-sentence and looking off into the distance, which made you believe she was thinking dark and dangerous things. But her directors didn't put this down to highly developed acting skills; they said that Mathilde Pelletier did this all the time because she was confused by the story or had forgotten her lines. Apparently she never understood anything about the films she was in because she only ever read her own parts of the script, and quickly forgot those too. Every action and piece of dialogue came as a real surprise, and that's why they called her First-Take Mathilde: the first take was the only one in which her reactions appeared real.

Hamish, the protagonist, is played by Julian Hadfield, a sullen, ex-Shakespearean actor known mainly from his work as a spoilt posh-boy-gone-wrong in TV shows like *The Saint* and *The Avengers*. He later crops up in *Columbo* and other American cop shows where his foppish insouciance, soft features and, at the end of the seventies, long fluffy hair, stood in for the corrupt debauchery of the idle rich.

The most quoted lines from the movie are from the earlier scenes where Eva, or Peanut as she is known at first, meets poor Hamish in the Hollow Egg café.

It's a game, Hamish, only a game.

Can I win?

Of course not. Play a game with me and you can only lose. But you can lose well or you can lose badly.

And if I lose badly?

You lose everything.

And if I lose well?

You lose only yourself. But maybe losing yourself is what you really want.

I took a can of Guinness out of the fridge, opened it, pressed play on the VHS, then sat down on the stacking chair to begin my journey, hoping the tape wouldn't get tangled up in the heads, or snap even, as it must have been worn very thin in certain places where I had replayed particular scenes over and over. There was a loud phut from the speaker then a curl of visual static on the screen and then, because I had taped it off BBC2 late one Friday night, the last notes of the theme tune to Patrick Moore's *Sky at Night* astronomy programme burst in, then faded away almost as quickly, to be followed by the continuity announcer.

And now it's time for our late film, Out of the Dark.

Silence.

A black screen.

The sounds of a city fade up.

It is night.

A car appears, moving towards us, and we quickly realise it is a police car. Then, in some deftly clever quick cut, the car is moving away from the camera, not towards us. We see its blue flashing light. It is speeding through dark city streets. And, as Raymond Chandler said, the streets seem dark with something more than night.

The brash orchestral dissonant music kicks in here, sounding wobbly and a little out of tune as if it had been mastered on to optical celluloid from tape. The discordant brass stabs and swelling atonal strings immediately identify the soundtrack as an important part of the film, and not to be ignored.

The car passes under a bridge that says *Senior Service* in big letters.

Then, over this car's urgent journey through the middle of some dark lonely city we know not where, the titles begin:

> *Associated British Pictures Organisation Presents*
> *A Hammer Film Production*
> *In Hammerscope*

Then on the left of the screen:

Mathilde Pelletier

and

Julian Hadfield

in

Out of the Dark

The words *Out* and *Dark* larger than the others.

The car sweeps past a roundabout and the famous

Rotunda building in Birmingham city centre swings into view – *Ansells, The Better Beer* in big letters low down on the side.

The names of the other actors and the makers of the film slide up in neat groups of three:

Patricia O'Shea

Maureen Fleming

Roger Hare-Duke

Then:

Screenplay by Ted Betteridge

Based on the novel The True Confessions of Eva X *by Roger Knight*

Music composed and conducted by Alan Smithee

Recorded by the Associated British Studios Orchestra

Recording Director Oswald Nairn-Watkins

The director of photography, the art director, and the supervising editor get a mention.

Then there is a close-up of the back of the heads of the driver and the other passengers as the dark city flashes past.

Brightly lit-up shop windows, pubs and bars.

Signs saying *Capstan* and *Smoke Bewlay Pipes.*

Then, on the titles, the rest of the crew's names roll by – from production manager down to casting directors – and just as the car screeches to a halt outside a restaurant, the final credits slide in.

Costumes by Bellmans

Contemporary furniture by G Plan

And the film begins in earnest.

I played the film from start to end – only one hour and twenty-seven minutes (films were a lot shorter then) – and then I sat and thought about it as I looked at the wall. I thought that the answer would have been obvious. I thought

I would have seen it immediately right in front of me, there, looming like a planet. But no. Nothing I had seen or heard seemed to fit the bill. The job required a detailed forensic viewing with careful notes and even, possibly, some freeze-frames and slow motion. Maybe a listen to the soundtrack without the images, from the cassette tape we'd made.

This job, I realised, was going to take a few days, even weeks. And I was not sure how long I had before I was needed back in west Cumbria.

I opened the doors to the balcony and went outside to look at the motorway intersection. I think that most other Cumbrians would have hated the idea of living right next to a motorway intersection, but to be honest, this was one of the things that appealed to me about the address.

I watched fascinated as six lanes of the M6 packed with trucks and cars and coaches and vans merged with six similarly crowded lanes on the M5 and marvelled at the looping slip roads, the underpasses, the overpasses, the fabulous feat of engineering that made the whole thing possible.

The letterbox rattled and I knew it wasn't the wind. At first I ignored it, but it rattled again, and this time there was a somewhat irritated manner to its tone – if a clanging of metal can have that quality. After a short pause, it went again – insistently, urgently this time – and I sensed that it was not going to stop, so I went to the door and threw it open in a furious manner ready to speak my mind to the unwelcome caller.

A small child was standing there, a girl, and she was laughing, as if at a joke someone who was no longer present had told her before running away. She laughed with a strange shushing sound like compressed air.

She stopped laughing but continued to smile at me. 'The woman in number 67 would like to talk to you,' she said.

'Oh,' I said. 'What's her name?'

'We call her Agnes. That's what she said to call her.'

'So that's her name. Agnes.'

'I don't know. But that's what she said to call her.'

The little girl was dressed in heavy jeans with large turn-ups, a thick jumper like a fisherman might wear, and a plastic apron with a drawing of a chicken on it. I thought it odd to see a child in an apron, I don't know why. The apron was not very clean, but the rest of her looked reasonably well cared for. Her skin was pale and blemish-free and her hair was blonde and fresh-looking, and pulled back into a ponytail at the back as if she had many practical things to do and couldn't have it getting in the way. Sticking out of her jeans pocket were some clear plastic gloves, the type doctors use for examining people. She was holding a toy scooter patterned with zebra stripes.

'What about you? What's your name?' I said.

'My name is Betty.'

'OK, Betty,' I said. 'Where's your mum live, Betty?'

'My mother's called Margaret Fleming and she lives in number 46 but she never comes out because she's sick. She gets benefits – which she's entitled to – and I have to go to the post office and cash the cheques because she can't do it herself. I'm only twelve but I've been given the right. If you cut me in half I'd be half adult and half child. There's a carers' group that meets up on Wednesdays and I sometimes go to it. It's very boring but they say it's important to keep your links with the outside world.' She laughed her soft shushing laugh again, maybe at the fact that she was aware of how grown-up she sounded for a twelve-year-old. The soft hiss of her laughing made me wonder whether she had been told off at some point for laughing too loudly and had developed this almost silent way of doing it.

'Have you got someone to care for, Mr Quinn? Because if you did you could come to the carers' group too.'

I paused for a few moments and thought about the question. She looked at me without saying anything else.

'How do you know my name?' I said.

'Agnes told me it. I like it. I like the name Quinn. Sounds like someone brave from a fairy story. Someone who is going to save people.'

'Right,' I said. 'And she wants to talk to me?'

I squinted into the blackness of the corridor behind her.

'Agnes is stuck in bed at the moment because she had an accident. That's why she sent me to get you. She can't go out on her own. She can't go to work at her job at Bluebird, the toffee factory. The Bluebird factory is quite a long way away. Her job there is to manage the cars in the fleet. She is quite important, I think. Quite high up. There are over twenty-five cars to manage.'

The child's accent sounded as though she had learned to speak by watching posh children in adventure serials on the BBC, but there were burrs and flat ays in her accent too, like she had another voice hidden below the one she was using with me.

'Toffee,' I said. 'Sounds like she will know what to do in a sticky situation.'

Betty smiled and laughed her shushing laugh again, but this time it seemed polite, as if she was a machine laughing.

'Can you follow me,' she said. 'She's just over the way at number 67.'

Betty swung her scooter round, put her foot on it and

glided away across the corridor swiftly until she came to the open door of number 67.

'I have him, Agnes,' she called in through the open door of the dark flat. 'I have him here. Mr Quinn. See you later, navigator,' she said towards me, and then scooted off.

I entered the flat slowly as if I expected there to be a pit with spikes in it waiting for me on the threshold.

A weak voice said, 'In here,' and I followed it into the bedroom.

The curtains were closed and there was no light on, but I could see a human shape sitting up in the bed, and as I grew more accustomed to the dark, I could make out the shape of a woman's head and shoulders with a shawl over them. The woman flipped on a bedside lamp, but even then I couldn't really see her face properly because she was wearing a black furry beret tugged down low and giant oval black sunglasses with swooping curves on the sides like the fins of an American car. Her face looked dented on one side, and the skin I could see was dark blue and violet and brown and red and yellow, like she'd been dipped in different colours of paint.

'Thanks for coming,' the lady said. 'I asked Betty to fetch you because there's something I wanted to know.'

The voice that came out of her was a surprise – a low rasping noise as if parts of the throat that were not normally used for speech were rubbing together like rusted cogs.

'How did your accident happen?' I said.

'A bad fall owing to a pair of cheap fur mules.'

I looked about the floor to see if I could see the offending mules, but found only a pair of scuffed black ballet pumps.

Agnes looked at me looking. 'Normally I am a heels girl, heels all the way. See this leg?' she said, indicating her plaster-encased limb. 'There are big metal pins all through it.

The X-rays look like the insides of a robot.'

Her general bent-up posture, and the slow, careful move-
ments she made with her arms and hands while she spoke,
made it look as though the violence of her accident hadn't
stopped and that she was still in a state of motion from its
enormous energy. But, despite her injuries, she appeared to
be striving to maintain a degree of style: the red dressing
gown with its leopard-print fur collar and the large glinting
silver earring in one ear. An Elastoplast covered her other
earlobe, making me think that the piercing had been torn
in the accident. Her hair was tucked up into the furry beret, except for one straggly end which was stuck to her face
with dark congealed matter which looked like blood. Her
lips were badly swollen, and bore the marks of healing cuts.

'So I fell, Mr Quinn. Simple as that. I hadn't even been
drinking, nor had I been drinking the night before. It was
early morning, the lift was out of order, and I was on my way
out for bread. That's the one thing I have to have fresh in the
morning and the local shop get me a baguette in every day.
They don't normally stock baguettes – it's mainly custard
tarts and big white sliced loaves – but they agreed to get one
every day especially for me. I am the sort of person who people do favours for. I don't really know why. Ever since I was a
little girl I found that if I asked for things to be a certain way,
usually things would be arranged the way I had suggested.
Anyway, that morning I tossed a coat over my nightwear and
when I reached the stairs the mules went one way and I went
another. Concrete is unforgiving. Look at me now. A horrible sight. Can you pass me those cigarettes, please? And the
matches. And then light one for me and put it in my mouth?
That's a darling. I was just wondering whether a man called
John Ireland had been round to see you.'

'I don't know,' I said. 'What does he look like?'

'A big, capable-looking man with crooked teeth.'

'No. No one's been round yet. You're the first resident of Acacia Avenue I have met. After little Betty,' I said.

She took a long draw on her cigarette and blew smoke out of the side of her broken lips. 'He'll come round, John Ireland, and he'll ask you if he can rent out your garage.'

'Oh.'

'There's a row of garages just out there. You must have seen them. One of them is yours, by rights. But John Ireland, he will want to sublet it off you.'

'What should I say?'

'Well, it depends on whether you want to sublet your garage or not.'

I had noticed the set of garages at the top of the road, their doors painted in a lustrous black gloss. They presented an intimidating blank wall of wood to walk past every day, if you were going in that direction, which most people were because it was on the way to the nearest bus stop. I wondered whether Mathilde Pelletier had been affected by this black wall as she walked past it on the way to filming, whether it had influenced the mood of the film.

'Who is John Ireland and why does he want my garage?'

'He lives in the other block. He's now got the other seven garages and we think – this block thinks – that he wants all eight,' said Agnes.

I thought it odd that 'this block' had thoughts – or rather that this woman, Agnes, imagined that the block had thoughts – and I wondered how she tuned in to them.

'Oh, OK,' I said.

'Yours will complete the set.'

'Did the previous owner not want to sublet it?'

23

'No. The previous owner of your place had some special old car. It's only people with valuable cars who need garages nowadays. It's the insurance.'

'What was the car?'

Agnes shrugged, then winced as if the shrug had caused her a spasm of pain. 'Something to do with a Sunbeam. From the sixties.'

'Nice.'

'I suppose. But you don't have a valuable car, do you?'

'No.'

'Well then, he'll definitely expect you to rent it to him.'

I wondered how I might use the garage if I kept it. I could store things in it. But my possessions consisted of video cassettes of old films, old film soundtracks on second-hand vinyl, and books about old films. These items would not fare well in a damp garage. I really couldn't think of any use for it, and if the price was right I must admit I would be happy to rent it to anyone. I didn't even mind what he wanted to use it for.

'Is it connected to the history of that flat?' Agnes didn't say anything and I stared at her for a long time and maintained the silence. 'It's rumoured that parts of a famous old film called *Out of the Dark* might have been filmed there,' I said, finally.

'No. John Ireland wouldn't know anything about that,' she said, with a strange, unfounded confidence that I thought a little odd. 'Anyway, I heard that those film people never used the garage, it was sublet to someone else at that time too.'

So it was true. It was the right flat.

'The caretaker told me about it,' she went on. 'I've only been here a few weeks myself.'

'These garages always seem to be getting sublet then.'

Agnes didn't comment on this remark.

'I let him have mine as well,' she said. 'Which you'd think was strange, with my job.'

'Oh?'

'I work at Bluebird, the toffee factory out in Romsley on the Halesowen Road. I look after the company cars for the sales reps. I'm the fleet manager.'

My mind drifted as she explained in great detail all about the role of a fleet manager at a large toffee factory.

I was in Cumbria, in the attic bedroom of my parents' house with its sharply sloping ceiling. Fiona was being sick and I was holding her hair away from her face and stroking her back. Out of the window I could see the bright lights of a bus rolling up the dark road from Whitehaven towards Cleator Moor. On the radio the future of obscure countries ending in *stan* was being discussed in a piece about the collapse of the Eastern Bloc. From downstairs I could hear the faint crackling purr of one of my mother's records, I think it was 'Release Me' by Engelbert Humperdinck.

'So that's me,' Agnes said, pulling me back to reality. 'The caretaker told me that these blocks are an elephants' graveyard for divorcees. Are you another casualty?'

'What?'

'Another one on the scrapheap?'

I thought about this question for a long time and it sent my mind in various directions which I was unable to follow completely, and I couldn't answer her.

'I really have to go,' I said.

'Well, keep me posted on John Ireland,' Agnes said.

Back in my flat I looked at the door buzzer and its dusty black wire going through the wall to the button on the other

25

side and wondered why Betty had flapped the letterbox rather than rung the bell. I thought about my mysterious new neighbour, Agnes. Something about this woman and her situation sickened me. The fact that she had survived whatever it was she had gone through, while others did not, made her a hateful figure who had been unfairly favoured over others and was unable to appreciate this fact. She was someone who focused only on her bad luck and not on her good fortune. And something about her didn't fit with these flats and this part of the world. Her injuries didn't look like they were from a fall, they looked more like injuries you would get from a beating – not that I had seen anyone in real life after a bad beating, but I had seen enough films and watched enough crime drama. Had she really fallen down the stairs? Or had she been beaten up? I thought about checking the stairs for spots of blood but stopped myself. I was living too much in the world of film noir. I was not here to get involved with other people's problems.

CHAPTER TWO

1988

I went out to the phone box on the other side of the grassy area and rang the number. All was the same, nothing was different, the bright female voice on the other end told me, after she had been sought from what sounded like some distance away. I was not to worry.

Through the window of the phone box I could see a group of kids near the entrance to the flats, and beyond them I thought I could see flames flickering on the green area and silhouettes of people jumping around. I wondered if they were burning a stolen car and dancing around it.

'Call again tomorrow, Mr Quinn. Call as often as you like and any time at all.'

I was impressed by the way she was always able to be both cheerful and serious at the same time, and I imagined that she had the ability to impart all kinds of terrible truths and devastating information in the same polite and carefully measured tones.

Back at the flat, I went into the kitchen and took a can of Guinness out of the fridge. I didn't feel like watching anything on the TV. I wanted to keep my mind cleansed of any screen images apart from *Out of the Dark*. So the shows Fiona and I used to watch together – *Thirtysomething, Oranges Are Not the Only Fruit, The Life and Loves of a She-Devil* – none of these would have been appropriate.

With the TV off I could now hear all the noises that were coming from the flats and outside. I heard doors banging on the corridor. I heard the lift hissing open. I heard voices raised, a man's, then a woman's, maybe Agnes's. I heard shouting from down below in the street.

I dug out a record – Basil Kirchin's soundtrack to *The Abominable Dr. Phibes* – and put it on. Then I opened the door to the balcony and went outside.

It was very cold and I was glad I had my coat on. I stood supping my Guinness and looked out. The lights could be seen on the motorway, chains of hazy red and white blobs moving past one another. Ten o'clock at night and still busy.

I watched the traffic and thought about how different life was in a high-rise flat looking at a motorway compared to life back in Cumbria. I thought about how these two motorways seemed to connect me to the whole country. Not far below this intersection the M6 tangles with the A38 and the A38M at Spaghetti Junction and then goes on to the M1, M40 and M42, heading to Newcastle, Oxford and London, and even out towards the east, although this was only via 'A' roads.

A line of red lights was waiting to merge, white lights flashing past in the other direction. Trucks, motorbikes, coaches, vans. I wondered where they were all going and why they couldn't just stop rushing about and stay at home. I thought of the drivers looking over at my block of flats and seeing the lights in my window. They might be wondering what people were doing in these homes, lit up like illuminations for the entertainment of the motorway users. Perhaps the drivers would be envious. Perhaps they would wish they were snug at home in a flat watching the traffic rather than stuck in the thick of it, hardly moving. They would be able to see shadows and silhouettes. Movement. Maybe they would see me watching. But it wasn't like watching trains where you felt the need to communicate your presence. I never waved to them or gave away the fact that I was watching. Another swig from my Guinness and it was nearly gone, and I went to get another. I put on a different record, the volume low so as not to draw attention to myself or bring someone over from another flat to complain about the noise.

Scritti Politti's *Songs to Remember.*

I often used to play this record when I was on my own, before I met Fiona. I liked the lonely yearning quality of it. Yet I had never considered myself lonely and I had never felt lonely. I didn't believe that just being alone made you lonely. But now, for the first time in my life, I really felt as though I was on my own.

Scritti Politti ended and I put on Holger Czukay's *On the Way to the Peak of Normal.* Another favourite when I was in an introspective mood.

I went outside on the balcony again, but this time I wanted to sit down.

There was an opaque reinforced glass panel at the edge of the balcony about five foot high, so you could only see over it if you were standing up. I studied this problem for a long time. Then I got the tall stool out of the kitchen, lay it on its side, and balanced the stacking chair on that. Now I could sit up high and watch the motorway intersection while drinking my beer.

I got another Guinness, my fourth if you are counting,

and I played more records. It was now midnight. The motorway intersection had begun to thin out and the traffic was moving faster. At this time of night there were more trucks and fewer cars. The sound made by the motorway was interesting. It wasn't engine sounds, it was the friction of the wheels, a constant thrumming of rubber on tarmac.

A small, bright orange van stopped on the off-slip road and very soon a long line of cars had formed behind it because one of the lanes had been coned off for roadworks. Even at this time of night the combination of a blocked lane and a vehicle stopping appeared to be causing commotion.

I watched the driver of the small van get out and then walk down the side of the van and to the back, where he appeared to check the doors. He examined the road behind the van as if checking to see whether anything had fallen out then he waved to the queue of cars behind as if by way of apology, returned to his bright orange van, and moved off, allowing the traffic to flow freely again.

A few minutes later the bright orange van entered the Yew Tree Estate and parked in front of the garages.

The words JOHN IRELAND were written on the side.

It was the name of the man who was likely to want to rent my garage.

I couldn't help wondering whether John Ireland had stopped his van on the motorway deliberately because he suspected I would be watching and he wanted me to see his van, to see his name, John Ireland, in large print in a public place, to see that he was someone important.

I went back inside, shivering as I hit the comparative warmth of the interior of my flat. I had a job to do. The light on the VCR was flashing because it had been paused. I stopped it and then pressed rewind. The tape fluttered and whined, growing higher in pitch as it reached the end of the spool, and then made a loud plastic clunk when it stopped.

I pressed play and sat down to watch the film in a more detailed and forensic way, a pen poised in my hand over a pad, so I could note down anything that might help me in my search.

After the title sequence where the police car is racing through the streets of late-night Birmingham, the car stops outside a restaurant and the policemen jump out. We cut to an interior, a man lying prone on the floor, blood seeping out from under his splayed raincoat. He is face down so we can't see who he is. A phone is ringing insistently. There are more police sirens in the distance.

Then, an abrupt cut, and the entire screen is filled with an immense tightly framed shot of a woman's eyes. Pull back to reveal it's a glamorous blonde, pull further back to show that her hands are in the air, then pull even back further to show that a gun is pointing at her.

The man pointing the gun is nervous, sweating, shaking.

It is our hero, Hamish McGrath.

Cut back to the glamorous woman. Her face is mostly in shadow, we don't see her features. Then the camera slides away from her face and begins a slow pan around the restaurant. We see signs of a scuffle – tables upended, chairs on their sides, plates on the floor with food spilling off them on to the carpet, wine glasses smashed. There are jackets on the backs of chairs, but there is no sign of anyone else in the room.

Cut to the view of the window from outside, then to a policeman in a van holding a phone connected to a large radio receiver. A suffocating silence seems to envelop the interior of the van. Then a cut to the policeman's point of view, the restaurant window. Street noise, sirens, low talking. There then follows one of the film's most famous shots, much discussed in cinema journals: a slow 360-degree pan which gradually reveals the whole exterior scene. We see that the place is surrounded by police officers crouching with guns pointed at the restaurant. Behind this line, waiters, chefs in checked trousers, and couples and groups of smartly dressed people without coats are being interviewed by the police. The 360-degree pan continues until we are back at the restaurant window. The sound of the phone ringing becomes louder in the mix and the camera goes towards the window and then seems to melt through the glass and we are back into the room. This is an effect employed by Hitchcock in *Psycho* and Orson Welles in *Citizen Kane*.

Keeping the gun on the woman, Hamish walks to the counter where the phone sits, and he answers it. He sits down and motions for the woman to sit down also and she does. Keeping the gun trained on her, he begins to tell his story to the person on the end of the phone. As he tells the story the camera zooms in slowly on to his hand, the coiled telephone cord wound tightly around it.

It all started when I met this dumb little nothing of a waitress at a greasy spoon on the Bull Ring, Birmingham.

Cut to a close-up of the radio in a police car, a needle on a dial flicking up and down in time with Hamish's voiceover.

Then dissolve to a café sign, the Hollow Egg, and cut to the café interior, where a plain-looking woman is cleaning tables. She wears glasses and her mousy hair is pulled up severely into a ponytail.

Hamish's voiceover:

I used to call her Peanut because she offered me one once. She wasn't beautiful, she wasn't sexy, she wasn't smart. But there was something about her and I used to go in there, the Hollow Egg, and flirt with her at every opportunity. And she flirted back. Me and Florence weren't getting on so well back then, and I was using the Hollow Egg as a place to escape to. Me and Peanut, we got to chatting a lot – jokes about how some day we'd run away together. It was all very light-hearted, you know how it can be. Then one afternoon…

DISSOLVE

Hamish is sitting at a table in the Hollow Egg writing numbers into boxes on a piece of headed paper. A close-up of the document shows the words *Hamish McGrath, Assistant Chief Accountant, The British Motor Corporation, Longbridge Plant, Birmingham.*

A line of smoke rises from a cigarette in the ashtray.

Peanut, the plain-looking waitress, appears behind him and slaps her hands over his eyes.

'More frothy coffee, Assistant Chief?' she says, moving to sit down in front of him.

'Is your frother working?'

'I can always get a froth up for you.'

On the jukebox 'Big Bad John' by Jimmy Dean is playing.

'Why don't you and I get together some time on a more tête-à-tête basis?' Hamish says.

'Mr McGrath, what can you mean?'

'Somewhere quiet. Where you can't hear bacon and eggs spitting in lard and old men coughing into their tea.'

'What on earth would we do in this private place? Wouldn't we get bored?'

'Oh, Peanut. Do you want me to draw you a picture?'

'No – but I will if you like?' She leans over, grabs his letter, spends a few moments drawing something on the back of it, then hands it back.

Hamish stares at what she has drawn.

His face becomes sweaty and he does the clichéd thing of running a finger around his shirt collar. We cut to a very quick shot over Hamish's shoulder but the camera is discreet, and somehow manages to avoid showing the full detail of her drawing. During this period of film-making in England, directors were coy about sexual content. By that time, 1962, very few films had any nudity in them at all. Michael Powell's *Peeping Tom* in 1960 was considered extremely daring and *Blow-Up* in 1966 was the first mainstream film to show pubic hair. By 1968 we had *Barbarella* and *Candy*, both considered risqué; on the arty side, we had experimental movies like Warhol's *Flesh*. But there was nothing in the mainstream. So the chances of the director of *Out of the Dark* giving us a full shot of Eva's drawing and getting it past the censor were slim. Later, a few people who saw it in the cinema will claim that the shot showed exactly what the drawing was of, in the same way that people remember the shower scene in Psycho as if it was in colour. But if you move through it frame by frame, you see just a few blurred lines. So during the whole film we never see anything at all of what the drawing actually depicts. But we know from Hamish's reaction and from Eva's facial expression, that it must be something powerful, daring, provocative and probably sexual.

Peanut parts her lips, licks them, then rests her hand on a plastic tomato-shaped sauce dispenser, rubbing the nozzle between her thumb and forefinger.

Many have mocked these clunky sexual metaphors – some critics even mentioned the *Carry On* series. Nevertheless, the scene is as erotic as the film gets and we see for the first time the potent sexual force that is the character of

Peanut/Eva. Slow, careful, controlling. Dripping ideas into Hamish's mind bit by tiny bit, so that he slowly accrues an immense and unconquerable desire for her that will eventually destroy him.

Hamish doesn't know what to do with himself. And this is when Peanut acts. She does something outrageous which will propel the action over the rest of the film. She grabs the drawing and, seeing a man sitting on his own nearby, stuffs it into the side pocket of the stranger's briefcase, then stares at Hamish with an outrageously cheeky look on her face.

Hamish looks at the stranger, then back at the waitress. He can't believe what she has done. But Peanut just puts on her coat and leaves and we see her outside, silhouetted by the bright afternoon sun, lighting a cigarette.

Hamish leaves the café and goes outside to her.

'You can't leave that drawing in there,' he says. 'It has the company name and my name on it too. As well as your effort at being Picasso for a day.'

'Too late,' she says.

The café's door flies open and the man with the briefcase barges past them roughly and marches off up the road – Eva's erotic drawing tucked away in his bag.

Lines from the song on the jukebox leak out:

No one seemed to know where John called home
He just drifted into town and stayed all alone

Hamish walks off quickly after the man. Peanut glances at her watch, then she pulls her ponytail even tighter than it is, tucks her heavy mumsy-looking handbag under her arm, and trots after him.

Shots of her flat, practical shoes landing in puddles. Mud splashing up on her thick, knobbly tights. Her heavy tweedy skirt swinging. Her thick coat buttoned up high. She seems at this stage like a woman who sees clothes only as useful items to keep her warm and protect her from the grime of the city streets.

She catches him up and, as if to steady herself, grabs his arm and they walk quickly together. There is a tight shot of her from Hamish's point of view, her face angled up to his, and we see that under the severity of her clothes and her square, metal-rimmed glasses, she is pretty.

They stop at a road junction.

'Fifteen years, five months, three weeks and two days in accounts down the drain,' says Hamish. 'I thought I recognised that bloke. It's Miles Dawson, our lovable shop steward.'

Cut to the shop steward disappearing off into the distance.

'A big troublemaker. Hates management and hates people like me from accounts even more.'

A shot of Peanut's face showing no expression. Then the music swells up, and the camera tilts sideways to reveal a stunning industrial panorama: two gasometers next to a cluster of cooling towers, a giant electricity pylon in the foreground, and all under a sky that is quickly filling with black clouds that could be either smoke or bad weather.

I paused the video there, finished my last Guinness and went to bed. I put on Radio 4 because I liked the soft brown tone of it, and I lay there thinking of Fiona in my arms. I took a pillow and held it to me as if it was her. I got up and went over to my hold-all and from it took out the Jesus and Mary Chain T-shirt she used to wear all the time and put it on my pillow near my face. It smelt of her. I wondered how long the smell would remain and pondered whether there was a way you could fix the smell into the fabric, to make it permanent, the way you can fix a dye into a cloth or stabilise images on photographic paper.

I couldn't get to sleep despite the radio, despite the Guinness. I thought about the traffic moving along the intersection, merging and changing lanes in a balletic way, the red lights and white lights blurring into wavy lines behind them like trails of ribbon and this seemed to soothe my mind and I drifted off.

CHAPTER THREE

1988

When I woke up the radio had been on all night. We both used to like to go to sleep with the radio on. We liked to allow sleep to crawl up on us rather than have to pursue it. We liked the half-aware half-asleep state where the voices on the radio drift between reality and your dreams.

I had slept through the *Shipping Forecast*, the World Service, *Farming Today*, everything. It was 07.47. On *Thought for the Day* a vicar, or some other man of the cloth, was talking about bridges. An arch bridge is made up of two weak structures, he said, but these two weak structures together form a strong structure – precisely because of their weaknesses. Perhaps people are like that, the vicar said, but he didn't go into a lot of detail. He just said that sometimes we should recognise the weaknesses in each other, and see these weaknesses as a strength.

There was a can of Guinness next to the bed, three-quarters full.

If Fiona had been here there was no way she would have countenanced me taking beer to bed. Whenever I did this, I never finished it, just had a few swigs and then went to sleep and the rest was wasted. She couldn't see the point. If you're going to drink it, drink it before you go to bed, or don't open it at all. It makes the bedroom smell and it's such a waste, and it's there in the morning too.

She was right of course. Fiona.

But Fiona wasn't here.

I got out of bed and went to the grim bathroom which had a plastic pink-coloured bath and a white sink with a long crack through it that had become blackened with grease. I showered and cleaned my teeth and then I dressed in black jeans and a black T-shirt and black V-neck pullover and black Dr. Martens shoes and went into the living room for my black denim jacket.

I looked at the record sleeves all over the floor.

I had left the door to the balcony open and a freezing cold wind was blowing in. I put on my denim jacket and in the pocket found a plastic wristband with the name Quinn on it. The back of my throat went slack and my face felt as though it were melting and tightening at the same time.

I thought of how I had held her before we – before she – before.

Before.

I sat down on the sofa and stared at the record covers.

Once there was a before and now there is only an afterwards.

I looked at my watch. Then I went out on to the balcony and leaned on the rail. I watched the creeping queues of traffic, everything all clogged up again just as it was yesterday. How odd it was that all those vehicles were there, so close, just a few feet away from my balcony, up high on those giant slabs of road balanced on fat concrete stems. I thought about how, if all the traffic stopped, actually stopped, and there was nowhere for it to go, and you literally couldn't drive anywhere, how difficult it would be to get out of your car and walk away. How would you get down to the ground? How would you get off these high sections of road without having to walk right down the whole length of them?

I took out the wristband again and looked at it, then I felt weak and quivery and put it back in my pocket.

I wondered whether I should eat some food before I went out. I wondered if I was looking after myself properly. Men left to fend for themselves don't look after themselves properly. That was what people always said.

I went back into the bedroom, lifted up the can of Guinness, and took it into the kitchen. On the cooker was a pan filled with cloudy grey water, gobbets of cooked egg white floating in it. A plate with crusts of toast on it sat next to an unwashed knife and fork on the kitchen top. A bottle of hot chilli sauce, Encona, had been left out on the table.

I looked at all this as if it were the remains of someone else's late-night meal not my own. I poured the beer into the sink, wincing at the nauseating stale smell of it, and watching the froth as it gathered around the plughole.

As I was walking through the hall towards the living room there was a loud assertive knock on the door.

I froze where I was and listened. I could hear breathing and shuffling.

The person knocked again and I went over to the door and leaned against it, thinking.

I could feel a thin gust of wind from under the door on my bare ankles.

Another knock came and then a voice.

'Hello? It's John Ireland. About your garage.'

I sighed and relaxed. John Ireland. The orange van. The

garages. I opened the door. John Ireland was a tall man, and wide, like a rugby player, with ruddy skin that looked soft. I noticed the crooked teeth that Agnes had told me about.

'I wondered if you wanted to sublet your garage,' he said.

'I'm not sure,' I said.

'Well, if you're not sure,' he said, 'have a think about it. I'll pop round again in a couple of days.'

'How much are you offering?'

'Well, the going rate is £25 a month. So how about that, plus a one-off payment of £200 as a sweetener?'

'Right,' I said.

There seemed no harm in it and the money was attractive. But I decided I would take the option of the couple of days he had offered me to think about it.

Later on, after telephoning the hospital again, I explored the area a bit more. I walked past the row of black garages and stopped at the end of the street, where it met a dual carriageway that continued in a long straight line all the way down into the centre of West Bromwich.

I crossed the road and went into a small park where there was a group of middle-aged women playing crown green bowls. I watched them for a time. Then I went over to a rundown-looking leisure centre with metal shutters over the windows. A gaudy mural had been painted on its walls, depicting smoking mill chimneys and industrial scenes, a bit like a seventies hippy version of a Lowry painting. Behind me, an old woman on a small electric mobility scooter went past with a large grass-cutting vehicle driving close behind her, trying to overtake. She pulled to the side and let the large vehicle pass, waving at its driver as he accelerated away. Then, when he had gone, she continued towards the main road, heading, I assumed, for West Bromwich town centre, which, considering it involved taking a powered wheelchair down a dual carriageway, seemed like a difficult journey to embark on.

I went back to the row of black garages. They looked abandoned, as if no one had ever opened them during their whole existence. I wondered why they were all painted black, and not different colours to reflect the personalities of the different people who owned them. Then I remembered that they all belonged to John Ireland.

Apart from mine.

I walked across the grassy area to the phone box and called the hospital again.

This time I had to wait a long time. I could hear the ticking of heels going down a long corridor, female voices, the squeaking of trolley wheels. Somewhere underneath it all I thought I could hear the faint music that they played in the waiting rooms, usually Radio Cumbria.

If something had changed they would be discussing how to tell me about it. They would choose the words carefully, they would have been trained to do that.

My heart always beat faster when I was waiting like this, and I gripped the receiver so hard my knuckles went white.

The voice that came on the other end reassured me.

Everything was fine. I was not to worry. The direction of travel was good. It had been a stable night. 'Call back again any time, Mr Quinn, any time at all.'

By now it was nearly dark. In the middle of the grassy area shadows bobbed about in front of a faint light which might have been from a fire, or a torch, or the headlamp from one of the small motorbikes the kids tore up and down on.

*

The next morning the letterbox rattled again. This time when I opened the door and looked down at Betty's tiny little frame I realised that she rattled the letterbox because she couldn't reach the doorbell.

'Agnes wants to see you again, Mr Quinn.'

'Will you take me round there again?'

'Compliance,' she said, and scooted off towards Agnes's flat with me following meekly behind.

'See you later, navigator,' she said when she left me at the door.

The bruises on Agnes's face had faded a little and she was out of bed, sitting in a chair at the dining table in the main room. She was still wearing her night attire and the red dressing gown, along with the furry beret. To this outfit she had added a scarf about her neck. The big black sunglasses were pointing towards the window and I followed her gaze. There was nothing to see except a silver Fiat Panda crawling up the slip road behind a removal truck. But through this window you could also see the garages, and I had an inkling it was those that she was watching.

The living room was sparsely furnished and everything was plain, dull and functional, as if it had been formed out of plywood by robots in Scandinavia. Two chairs, a table, a sofa and a portable television. A large screwdriver lay on the floor which I assumed she had used to put the furniture together. It looked as if she wasn't intending to stay in this place and there was nothing there that said anything about the personality of Agnes. Only one item in the room stood out – an old Super 8 film camera which she had placed on the mantelpiece as if it were an ornament. I wondered if she used it and made a note to ask her at a later date; I wasn't even sure if you could get that sort of film developed any more.

'Thanks for coming over,' she said. 'I enjoyed chatting to you last time.'

In the daylight streaming in from the window I could see that the swelling of her lips had reduced substantially, but I could also see that one of her cheeks bulged out dramatically as if she had a wad of chewing tobacco tucked in there. So her manner of speaking – that slow, blurry, indistinct rasping – seemed to be because she could hardly move her mouth and was forced to generate words from places she didn't normally use. Now that I could hear her better, I noticed that she had an unplaceable foreign accent which gave every utterance a dramatic feel like the spoken part of a foreign song.

'Sit down, sit down.'

I sat on the chair next to her, facing the window in the same way.

'I enjoyed our chat the other day. It's funny. I feel as though I know you already, Mr Quinn. Or can I call you Daniel?'

'Well, people call me Dan. They never call me Daniel.'

'I don't like the name Dan. It's too short. You couldn't sing it in "Happy Birthday", for example. How do they sing "Happy Birthday" to you?'

'They sing the whole thing. They sing Daniel. Dan-ee-ell.'

'Exactly. They know what they are doing, those people. I think that I shall call you Quinn. Your surname. I like the sound of it better. It's tough-sounding. Makes you sound like a tough guy.'

'That's fine. Quinn is fine.'

She picked up a packet of Gauloises and tapped out a cigarette.

'You know those bastards at Bluebird?' she said.

'The sale reps? The ones who use your cars?'

She lit her cigarette, took a long pull on it and blew smoke out of the side of her mouth.

'Betty took a phone call. I don't have a phone in here – Betty's mum is the only one with a phone on these top three floors. The call was from Howard Rifkin, one of our reps. Rifkin covers Bristol, the South West and most of Wales. He was very angry and little Betty wrote it all down, she's such a great kid. What's with this shit Sierra, Howard Rifkin says. No wipers on the headlamps? No heated front windscreen? That's what he says to little Betty. Tell that woman from me, he says to her, to little Betty, tell that woman, that Agnes, tell her that it's just not acceptable. And these features, Quinn, these extras, they are not about the functions themselves. Oh no. They are about status. That's all. Nothing else but pure status. This Howard Rifkin fella drives samples of toffee up and down the motorway. That's what he does for a living. That is his life. Yet he tells me that a salesman's car is his *castle on wheels*. My car, he says, is a symbol of the company's quality and the quality of the product. It is also a symbol of the quality of the man inside the car, the man who drives it. It is, put simply, the sum total of what I, Howard Rifkin, am worth to Bluebird, and to the world.'

I laughed. 'He sounds like a treasure,' and she laughed with me, but with some difficulty, eventually causing herself to have a coughing fit which meant I had to pass her a glass of water.

'And little Betty wrote all that down in a message?' I said, while I waited for her to regain the power of speech and continue the tirade against her employer.

'More or less. She got the gist of it and, to be honest, I

have added a bit of colour. I am a storyteller, Quinn, as you will learn. Howard Rifkin and all of those dim-witted bozos at Bluebird, they don't seem to care that I am a sick invalid, stuck in here, unable to do anything. All they care about are their shit tin boxes. This is a temporary job for me, Quinn. I'm not the sort of person who manages a fleet of cars at a toffee factory. It's a stopgap.'

I was about to ask her what it was a stopgap between and wondered about the old Super 8 camera on the mantlepiece. Maybe she knew a bit more about *Out of the Dark*. But I never got the chance to ask because she continued with her character analysis of sales rep Howard Rifkin, and I drifted off.

I thought about Cumbria, about Whitehaven. After it happened I drove around the one-way system over and over again for what must have been an hour. Then I swung off down to the docks and parked at the top of the hill. I looked out at the grey, swirling Irish sea, the waves frothing up against the long thin piers, the knots of fishermen on the ends.

Fiona had complained about the headaches and other symptoms for weeks but no one had understood.

The toffee salesmen were obsessed with status and status was defined by their cars.

Further out on the water I could see a large ship, a smudge of grey on the horizon, waiting a long way out. It would be holding chemicals for the Marchon plant. Small boats went in and out between the bigger ship and the docks to load and unload these mysterious substances.

Fiona had said she could hear a rushing sound in her head all the time, pounding and pounding, but she just got used to it.

The amount of toffee you sold dictated your position in the hierarchy.

On the docks was an enormous hopper attached to a chute that took what looked like roughly ground powder into the boats or out of the boats, I never knew which. At Donnan's Quay, a boat was in and men in donkey jackets and high-visibility vests were unloading boxes of wriggling silver fish.

My parents' giant, hard-backed medical encyclopaedia said it might be hay fever – the swelling of the face, the fluid retention in the feet, the headaches. But this was in the middle of winter.

A VW Golf parked up next to me really close, even though the car park was empty but for me. The driver and his female passenger began to eat chips they'd probably got from Rileys in the town and their windows became steamed up so they wound one down, making an electric *duzz* sound.

I thought about the way the hospital staff worked the bed controls, the motors softly whining as the bed tilted up and down.

The amount of toffee sold dictated the size of your car, its model, its engine power, and the number of extras.

A shadow of clouds moved slowly across the grass, and the sky changed colour. It was as if a violet-tinged greyness was seeping up into it from out of the sea. Three o'clock and it was already growing dark.

The days between then and now seemed thicker, like heavy solid slabs.

I faded back in.

'Sell a large amount of toffee and you eventually become a team manager, which means all the team's sales of toffee belong to you. And that's a lot of toffee, a lot of status, meaning a bigger and better car from little old Agnes.' She pointed to her chest with her thumb. 'That's me.'

I was listening to her speaking but not to the words. I liked the sound of her croaky voice and could lose myself in it without paying attention to the content. I wanted her to go on talking at me, reciting lists of luxury features that the sales reps wanted on their cars. I could happily sit there all day, leaning against her brown, crinkly voice as if it was a wall.

When she finally stopped speaking, there was a long silence and it took me some time to resurface from my reverie.

'You wanted to ask me something?' I said.

'Oh yes,' she said. 'I wondered if John Ireland had been round yet.'

'Yes. He's been round.'

'Oh.' She leaned forward towards me and squinted into my face. 'And?'

'And what?'

'The garage. Did he ask you about the garage?'

'Yes,' I said.

'And what did you say?'

'I am taking some time to think about it.'

She turned away from me and looked out of the window, over to the garages. She took another long drag on her cigarette, then turned back to me, and tried to smile, but her swollen cheek and lacerated lips wouldn't allow it. 'Do you think the man who built these flats took some time to think?'

'I don't know.'

'Or do you think he just went ahead and built them? He's a nice man, John Ireland, a good man. I get the impression that he hasn't had a good run of luck. It would cheer him up, I think, to have your garage and complete the set.'

When I got back to my flat, there was a letter on the mat. Strange, because no one knew where I was. It was unstamped, so had been delivered by hand, and the address was in a flamboyantly stylish hand with long swooping descenders and extravagant loops, like the handwritten titles you might see on the credits of an old film.

Mr Daniel Quinn
Flat 69
Tower 2
Acacia Avenue
Yew Tree Estate
West Bromwich
Warwickshire

It made me wonder why this block was Tower 2 and not Tower 1. And the use of Warwickshire, the old county name, was odd; this area had been known as the West Midlands since the early seventies as far as I knew. Also, there was no postcode on the letter, as if a postcode would have rendered the operation clumsy, as if making it ready to be understood by a machine would have demeaned its purpose.

I looked at it and wondered whether I should open it at all or just put it in the bin. Dealing with written communication was not something I relished. I struggled with reading when I was at school, and I still struggle with printed words. It might require a written reply and I have the same difficulties with writing as I have with reading. The letters look back to front and I spell words the wrong way round. It takes me ten times longer than the average person to produce a piece of written work, and it doesn't matter whether it's an essay, a letter, an administrative form, or even just a phone message. I have to keep doing it and redoing it, throwing it away, then starting again, then throwing it away again. Even when I'm done, I keep checking it and rechecking it before I'll let anyone see it.

It was film and the idea that you could actually study film like you would study a book that really opened things up for me.

Nevertheless I tore the envelope open and took out a small lined sheet of paper with handwriting on it and some figures.

Draft contract for the sublet of garage 0.07

£25 per month with £200 deposit

Signed by

And then two names, *Daniel Quinn* and *John Ireland*, with dotted lines next to them for signatures and the word *date* also followed by a dotted line. I put it back into its envelope and placed it on the mantlepiece.

I went back into the living room. I had to stop thinking about garages and the strange woman in number 67. I had a job to do. A film to watch. Somewhere in *Out of the Dark* was the answer to my problem and each time I watched it I found something new. So I would keep watching it over and over until the answer was clear.

I picked up the film at the point where Hamish is entering the famous Longbridge car plant. A sequence of external shots of the plant is followed by some medium shots of Miles Dawson, the shop steward, talking to a group of angry-looking men in overalls, clearly trying to calm them down. Miles Dawson is very different to the quiet, pensive Hamish. There is something dashing, dangerous, charismatic about him.

There follows a sequence of intercuts between Hamish and Peanut, all silent apart from Penderecki's brooding, muddy strings throbbing beneath it all.

Hamish in a glass office, looking at a ledger full of tiny handwritten figures, while behind him, men in overalls are smoking and laughing, presumably on a tea break.

Cut to Peanut in a baker's shop looking at small cakes. She holds up a single finger to indicate one only, and the man puts it into a paper bag.

Cut to Hamish in a meeting with other men in suits, while in the background, cars are rolling off an assembly line.

Cut to Peanut eating the cake on her own, staring at a blank wall in a shabby room.

Cut to Hamish at his desk, staring at a picture of himself standing in front of a caravan beside a drab-looking woman.

Cut to Peanut standing alone at the window of a high-rise flat, looking out over a motorway intersection. This flat. The flat that I was watching the film in now.

Each of these short scenes looks innocuous on the surface, but the heaviness of Penderecki's music imbues everything with an intense foreboding.

A big clock on the roof of the plant says 5.30.

Through the main gate, hundreds of men are leaving and Hamish waits across the road, pacing and smoking, scanning the crowds.

Then Peanut, in a long dark coat, flat shoes and plain headscarf hiding her hair, comes from behind him.

'Boo,' she says and Hamish visibly jumps.

'Where did you spring from?' he says.

'Everywhere and nowhere,' she says. 'Hey, look, there's your evil shop steward.'

Cut to Miles leaving the plant. He heads straight into a call box and Peanut and Hamish follow him. They stand outside the phone box as if they are queuing, and they hear him raising his voice.

'I know it's the second time this week, darling,' he is saying into the phone as the camera noses into his face. 'But I have a lot of issues on the shop floor… I know, I know. But you know how it is… yes… yes… the shop steward takes it from both sides. It's been a terrible week. I'll see you later.'

From what little we have seen of him, we are already aware that Miles Dawson has a moody disposition and a fiery temperament. He is played expertly by Roger Hare-Duke, known to English filmgoers from the Hammer Horror franchise where he had played a succession of scientists and investigators who usually met a bloody end in reel two at the hands of a vampire or werewolf. He has the look of a third-rate James Bond, with the sexual ambiguity of the omnisexual male – predatory, lustful, drug-drenched and perpetually aroused. This clever casting of Hare-Duke makes us suspect that Miles is not important to the plot, that he is reckless and his role won't last.

They follow Miles further. He buys flowers and a bottle of wine. He buys chocolates. They follow him into the station and on to a train, and this time he gets off at Solihull, where they follow him down a tree-lined street to a large Victorian house that has been converted into flats.

He rings a buzzer and looks up at a window. A young woman, much younger than he is, waves down to him. She is dressed in a fur-rimmed negligee and is wearing what looks like a turban. She smiles, then frowns when she notices Hamish and Peanut behind him, and Peanut and Hamish turn away and head off across the road.

They stop outside a large pub opposite the house.

They hear a clunk sound and turn to see the front door swing open and Miles go inside.

Hamish and Peanut go into the pub where they sit at the window and watch the house.

'What's your real name, Peanut?' Hamish says.

'Eva,' she says.

'Eva? Nice. You got another?'

'Another what?'

'Name.'

'Eva Ni Riain.'

'Wow.'

'Like Rain, but with an extra "i".'

'That's some fancy title.'

'Originally it was Ryan. Evaline Ryan. The Ni means born. I wanted to be a dancer for a while and I believed a new name would make me stand out.'

'Eva Ni Riain. It certainly does that. A dancer. And now you gyrate with the fried bread and sausages at the Hollow Egg. Will you dance for me some time?'

'I could. It's a skill that never leaves you. Muscle memory. Your body can do certain physical things without your brain getting involved.'

'There's a bus,' he says, 'in the city, called the number 11. It's famous. A circular route going all around the city all day long picking people up and dropping people off. I'd like to get on that bus and just stay on it all day. You know, watching the traffic and people getting on and off. Would you do that with me?'

Eva says nothing, just looks out of the window.

'Well, Eva Ni Riain, what do you think he is up to, this Miles Dawson?'

'You know what he is up to. He is up to what you would like me and you to be up to.'

'So now we know his little secret. Interesting, isn't it?'

'Why?'

'Just – you know – what with you and I?'

'I don't know what you mean.'

'Oh yes you do, little Miss Rain with an extra "i".'

At this point the camera tracks down to their feet and we see her shoe gently rubbing against his ankle, and Hamish's voiceover comes in again.

She had me by then, had me well and truly, like a gasping salmon wriggling on a line, and there was no way I was going to be able to get that hook out of my mouth and swim away. Eva Ni Riain had filled my senses and all I wanted was more and more of her and I felt at that point that there was nothing I wouldn't do to keep this woman near me.

I stopped the tape and thought about the voiceover.

Some people say that a film has failed if it needs a voice-over. A film should be able to tell the story by what is happening on the screen. But I like the voiceovers in film noir. I like the way that the voiceover could tell you something about the scene that you couldn't know from what you could see happening before you, and often it was something that the characters couldn't know either. Like *Little did they know but this was the last time the brothers would ever meet.* Only a voiceover could do that. I began to wish I had a voiceover accompanying my life and wondered what it would be saying at the moment.

It would be saying *I had been in the flat now for three days and I had no idea what had been happening back in west Cumbria where I ought to be and where I was most needed.* And then the voiceover would say *If I had known that, things might have been very different* and the film would cut to what was happening in west Cumbria at the time. But there was no voiceover and I couldn't have access to what was going on in west Cumbria. All I could do was call up on the phone twice a day and listen to the footsteps going down the corridor while I waited for the soft reassuring voice to tell me that everything was as it was when I left.

The wind was throwing rain against the window pane with a rattling sound. I turned off the TV and pressed the button that made the VHS cassette pop out and replaced it in its cardboard sleeve.

I went into the spare bedroom, rummaged in a box, and brought out a well-played music cassette, a compilation of up-and-coming unknown artists that had been given out free with the *New Musical Express*.

I stuck the tape in the stereo and rewound it for exactly seventeen seconds then pressed play.

A soft female voice over rudimentary strummed guitar chords, some bleeping, booping synthesisers, and a drum machine.

Resistance is futile
Nothing can help you now
I have you surrounded
You'll never get away

CHAPTER FOUR

1986

I first came across Fiona when I saw an alluring face on a poster for a gig by Pop Pop Pop!, an electro pop trio. Pop Pop Pop! were made up of a synth player, a guitarist/singer and a dancer. The dancer filled nearly the whole poster and was dressed in high silver boots and a red bobbed wig, and her gaze into the camera was a look that went right down into the depths of my heart.

The gig was in Walsall Town Hall and Pop Pop Pop! were low down on a bill in an afternoon festival that was headlined by Alien Sex Fiend, Cabaret Voltaire and Dead Can Dance. They were due on at 12.45 in the afternoon and I got there half an hour early and stood at the front and watched them sorting out their cables and amps and pedals, and the guitarist saying *one two* into the mike. The dancer, the member of the trio I was interested in, was wearing all black and had lots of dark make-up around her eyes, all Siouxsie Sioux really. But she had a lot of silver on too, like in the poster – silver dyed hair, a big silver thing the size of a dinner plate about her neck and little silver boots over tight black leggings that emphasised the length of her legs.

On her head she wore a small pillbox hat that was red and yellow with thin chains hanging off it.

Their set began with no announcement. The synth player, a serious maths graduate type, in an RAF great coat and big white plastic spectacles, set off a drum machine which went psst psst, click click click, then he made a few low rumbling noises with some other machine, and then started to pick out some bass notes on his Korg. His stage persona was stiff and his movements repetitive and awkward, as if he was one of those automatons that they have outside cobblers' shops, hammering invisible nails into boots while turning their heads from side to side and smiling. The guitarist played a simple repeating figure on the three lower strings, with an echo effect on it to thicken the sound, and put her mouth close to the mike and sang softly like an old-fashioned crooner.

Resistance is futile
Nothing can help you now
I have you surrounded
You'll never get away
Resistance is futile
There's nothing you can say
Now that you're in my corner
You'll have to stay

The dancer moved about the stage in an insouciant, sensual manner while the maths man played his synth nonchalantly with one finger, and the mousy singer at the back hushed and purred her way through the words, at times even turning her back to the audience. I liked them. They sounded a bit like Young Marble Giants, or early Human League. But the dancer was definitely the attraction for the audience as she swooped and dipped and careered about the stage like a large bird. I, like everyone else, was enthralled by her. And when I heard that she was living in Walsall it made her seem much more attainable than someone who lived in, say, Birmingham city centre. Watching her onstage that afternoon, dancing to the squeaky out-of-tune warblings of the mousy guitar player, I believed that I had fallen in love there and then. There is something about inept musicians that I am drawn to. Something fragile and imperfect, always reaching out but never getting there. And what could be more inept than someone who couldn't play anything at all – who just dressed up funny and scampered all over the stage making strange shapes.

Afterwards I hunted her down in the bar where she was speaking with the white-spectacled synth man and the mousy, quiet guitarist and I interrupted them to say how wonderful I thought the set was.

Then I lied. 'I'm knocking together a small festival myself,' I said, wondering why I had used the term *knocking together*, and assuming I chose it because it made me sound casual and masculine, like I was constructing a small building. 'To take place at Balloons Wine Bar in Walsall in a few months.'

'What's this festival called?' the maths man said while the dancer just stared at me.

'It will be called Gun Crazy,' I said, plucking a random film noir title out of my head.

'I like it,' she said, without smiling.

'Have you ever shot a gun?' I said.

'No,' she said, and put her hand up to her mouth and laughed. 'Why?'

'Don't worry, it's not strictly necessary,' I said.

At this point the synth player turned his back to us and moved closer to the guitar player. It sounded as if they were arguing.

'The problem is,' the dancer said, 'how would I get to this festival? Because I live in the real world, and I'm not sure how good the transport connections are between the real world and your imagination.'

I slowly negotiated the twists and turns of this sentence in my head before I realised she was making fun of me.

'Oh, here,' she said, smirking, and handed me a mandarin orange with a number written on the side in felt pen.

CHAPTER FIVE

1988

The wind pulled hard through the gap between the two towers. I walked quickly through it and on to the giant featureless expanse of grass opposite the tower blocks, feeling – as always when I was in the middle of this bleak and barren patch of nothingness – very exposed. I sometimes thought it might be better to move like a mouse and stick to the edges of a space, but it would have added a lot of time to my journey.

These flats were in an in-between place – neither in Walsall nor in West Bromwich but exactly halfway – so it was equally inconvenient to travel to either of the two towns. Getting to Birmingham city centre itself meant a long walk across the grass and then a longer walk to the main road, the A34, where you could get a 51 bus to the city centre through Perry Barr and Great Barr.

I went into the phone box and called the number again. All was OK, but the nurse asked me when I was coming back up that way and as I'd only been away a few days I was a bit surprised and wondered if there was something wrong, something she could only tell me about face to face.

I tried to tune in to the sounds of the hospital behind her – the chinking of metal, the humming of machines, voices chattering – but there were no clues.

'I can come right away,' I said. 'If you need me there. It takes three hours and twenty-three minutes on the train.'

'No, Mr Quinn, that really won't be necessary. Don't worry – there are lots of improvements. Everything is moving in the right direction. The doctors are really pleased.'

I waited at the stop and when a number 11 turned up I got on. I settled into a seat upstairs at the back and looked out of the window. The bus's circuit of the city took about three hours and I had all the time in the world. I needed some privacy for a while. And no one can find you when you are on a bus. It's impossible. Cars are traceable and identifiable, but on a bus circling the outskirts of Birmingham? It would be as if the ground had opened up and swallowed me whole. And maybe if I spent some time away from the film, maybe just a day, maybe I would approach it next time with a clearer mind and then I would better see what I was looking for.

And this journey was one I had taken with Fiona.

The number 11 was full of those people who waited for the off-peak period to get a cheap or free journey. The old people, the sick people, the young women with pushchairs. I noticed that people who travel on buses across cities or around them were very different to people who travel in and out of the centre. They have different purposes. People on orbital or cross-city buses are visiting relatives and friends who live in other suburbs, or going to work in out-of-town industrial or retail parks. For them, the city centre is not a place you go in and out of, but an inconvenient lump in the middle of the conurbation that you have to negotiate your way around. There were no students in these parts of Birmingham, none of the educated poor, or the middle-class dilettantes you get in the centres, edges and leafy bits of the big cities. This was the outer fringe, the real towns, the yet-to-be or probably never-to-be gentrified old settlements of the Birmingham conurbation.

We went though Sarehole Mill and into Kings Heath, and then had to wait for ages at a big junction in Cotteridge. I could see down into the cars next to us in the thick knot of traffic. A young woman was putting on her make-up using the car's vanity mirror; a man was tapping his steering wheel and bobbing his head to the radio. An older woman was surveying the heavy queue of traffic with quick jerks of her head as if she had to be somewhere really important and was looking for a way that her car could slide though the gaps.

At a bus stop I was surprised to see a small figure on the other side of the road that I recognised: little Betty from the flats. But before I had a chance to wave over, she had boarded a bus which said Worcester on the front. Worcester was a long way out of town and I supposed she would be getting off somewhere en route. However, we were nowhere near the Yew Tree Estate, and I wondered what she was doing so far away from home. Maybe she had relatives that she didn't talk about, or appointments in distant hospitals that she had to go to in lieu of her sick, housebound mother.

I looked out of the window at the sky. Blue and cloudless, no wind now. Some traces of frost remained on the corners of the bus window panes and condensation was building up on the inside where the hot breath of the bus's occupants met the cold glass. We rumbled through Bourneville, Harborne, Dudley Road, Perry Barr Island, down Aston Lane, round Swan Island. The bus vibrated as it pulled up the hard hill to Billesley then it went under a low-hanging tree, its branches pattering on the roof sounding like the cock-roaches scattering across the kitchen floor after the lights were switched on in our student house in Walsall.

I heard this sound three times before I decided that I had completed the circuit often enough.

CHAPTER SIX

1988

Betty rattled the letterbox only once this time, as if she knew by now that I would hear it easily and that several rattles would be irritating. She seemed very sensitive to other people's feelings, which must come from caring for her invalid mother.

'Have you arranged another audience with her majesty for me?' I said.

'Compliance,' she said.

'Well thanks very much and I will see you later, navigator,' I said as I walked over to Agnes's flat unaccompanied for the first time.

Agnes was lying on the sofa with the remote in her hand as if she had just turned off the television.

'Betty took another call from Bluebird.'

'Did she write it all down again?'

'Yes. They are carrying out a review at work.'

'Right,' I said, sitting down on the arm of the sofa near her feet, now encased in the famous fur mules. The bruises and swellings on her face were nearly gone and although she was still wearing the dark glasses and hat, the neck scarf had been discarded, so I could see her throat, which was long, slim and pale like a vase.

'And Vince, the big manager, he said to her, "The thing about her job, Agnes's job, is that it could be done anywhere. Her skills are completely transferable."'

'Harsh.'

'Yes. And Bluebird ought to be a company you can trust. It's a family firm that goes back a hundred years. There used to be a purpose-built village next to the factory. Pass me my cigarettes, would you, darling? They're in the bedroom.'

I found the cigarettes by the bed, and to be honest, I took a little longer in there than I needed as there were a lot of her clothes all over the place. Mostly black. I picked up a couple of items, unfolded them and had a closer look. There was a gauzy, transparent blouse with a long ribbon on the front and floaty sleeves shaped like bells. I pressed this garment to my face to see what perfumes I could pick up and got a rush of musk and chocolate and bitter herby stuff, followed by a darker smell like wet soil. I tried to process these odours to see if there was any information in them that would help me interpret her better, this strange woman with her weird job at a toffee factory, her slightly foreign-sounding accent, and her possibly invented accident. Then I replaced the blouse on the bed and went over to the dressing table. While every surface in the rest of the flat was bare and unoccupied, the dressing table was covered in tubes, bottles, brushes, powders, lipsticks, perfumes and ointments. I don't know why I did it but I picked up one of the lipsticks, took off the lid and drew some lips on the back of my hand. Then I placed the lips on my cheeks, leaving a kiss mark. I replaced the lid and put the lipstick in my pocket, wiped the self-inflicted kiss off my cheek with my fingers.

Back in the living room I handed her the cigarettes and she tapped one out of the packet, and offered me one too.

'I never took to it,' I said, shaking my head.

She lit up and continued. 'People have lived and worked at that toffee factory, Bluebird, all their lives. A woman told me that her grandparents met at a dance at the Bluebird concert hall, fell in love, and had their wedding do at Bluebird too. You could live, work, study, play, love, marry, have kids, and then die at Bluebird, all without ever leaving the site.'

As she spoke she waved her cigarette all over the place, making ash fly everywhere. Her voice was now almost normal-sounding – apart from the croakiness which I guessed was permanent from a lifetime of sucking down untipped French cigarettes.

'Who would manage all the cars?' I said.

'Exactly.'

'Twenty-five, Betty said.'

'Vince, the big boss, said to Betty, "Listen, tell Agnes this: the people who are close to the toffee, the people who make the toffee, and package the toffee, and sell the toffee, they really know their stuff. The different flavours. The pictures on the tins. The metal hammers. Everything like that. But you know what –"'

Agnes paused and looked at me for a long time.

'"Show me a toffee factory where the staff are too far away from the toffee and I will show you a toffee factory heading for problems."'

'That's what Betty wrote down?'

'That's what he said to her and that's what little Betty wrote down.'

The sun through the window had made white fuzzy

shapes on the floor and I stared at it. In Cumbria, Fiona had started to see zig-zag lines. Anything could set it off. Flickering lights, shadows, rows of vertical posts, certain patterns.

'Do you think I should leave this job now, or wait for this restructure?'

I told her what I knew about English employment law and sick pay, but she didn't seem to be listening because as soon as I had finished speaking, she said, 'Have you given your garage over to John yet? John Ireland?'

I didn't reply. Why should I tell this woman about my dealings with John Ireland?

'Oh,' she said, looking at my aggrieved face. 'That's interesting. Now I can tell when I've overstepped the mark. Now I know where the borders are, the outer limits.'

CHAPTER SEVEN

1988

Back in my flat I went into the bathroom and stood in front of the mirror. I took out the lipstick I had stolen from Agnes and drew a shape on the mirror around my head. It was the shape of a cloud because that's where I felt I was at that point.

I sat down in front of the paused VHS and pressed play. Hamish and Eva were still sitting in the pub watching the house that Miles Dawson had entered to meet the scantily clad young lady they had spied at the window.

Cut to Miles emerging from the young lady's house and then to Hamish and Peanut jumping up and supping down their drinks before running out of the pub.

They follow him again.

He goes down the street and round the corner and back to the station. He gets on a train and they do too, sitting down near him in the carriage.

Eva engages Miles in idle chat about the weather and while he is looking the other way, Hamish slips his hand inside the side pocket of his briefcase where Eva's erotic drawing has been tucked away.

But Dawson turns round.

'What the hell are you doing?'

'Sorry,' Hamish says, jumping up.

Dawson lunges at Hamish and Hamish pulls away from him. Then suddenly we have a close-up of Dawson's face and we know that all is not right. His hand leaps up to his throat and his eyes roll backwards. We realise that he is experiencing some sort of seizure and he rolls off the seat, and collapses on to the floor, drooling.

Close-up on Hamish looking worried, staring at the man on the floor.

Close-up of Dawson's hands twitching, then his feet twitching, then to his mouth with white foamy froth coming out of the side.

Eva acts quickly. She moves Miles into a safe recovery position and checks his mouth for obstructions.

'I had to do a first-aid course for the café,' she says.

She kneels by him, holds his hand, touches his throat, and seems to be counting. Then she stands up.

'He'll be fine now, he'll come round. Go and get the guard. He'll make sure there's an ambulance to meet him at the next stop.'

Hamish doesn't say anything for a long time, and the camera stays on his face, tracking in a little closer as if to indicate deep thought, as if we are trying to get into his head.

'What are you waiting for?' she says.

'They'll keep him in hospital and he won't want that. He'll want to get home to his wife.'

Hamish puts his hand into the man's bag again.

'You're not looking for that pathetic doodle again, are you?'

But instead of the drawing, Hamish pulls out an envelope and taps the address. 'I'll take him home.'

'What?' she says.

'Yes,' says Hamish. 'I'll take him home. Make sure he's OK. It's my fault.'

The train stops and Eva opens the carriage door.

'Count me out,' she says, 'I'm getting off here.'

Suddenly Hamish is alone with Miles. There is a long shot of the carriage, empty but for Hamish standing looking at Miles prone on the floor .

Cut to a close-up of Miles's face, his lips quivering, his eyes shut, his face screwed up as if in pain, his breathing loud and heavy. Then his eyelids begin to tremble and they suddenly open and he looks about him. His face seems to crumple as if he has discovered he has lost something important or has been shamed. He swivels his head about violently to take in his surroundings, then when he has ascertained where he is, his head slumps back again with a thud and he sighs deeply. He lies still, looking up at the carriage doors, saying nothing.

Cut to another long shot of the carriage and Hamish looking at him on the floor.

Cut to Miles's point of view from his place on the floor, through the glass doors as the train rattles along, the lights from houses, cars and street lamps streaming past making us think of the electric flashes in his brain when he had the fit.

Hamish's voiceover is played over this long abstract shot of the flickering, racing lights.

To be honest, at that point I was almost as interested in the man on the train floor as I was in Eva. He had a more exciting life than me, with his union battles and his illicit sexy young girlfriend. Maybe I wanted to find out how that way of living worked, find out if there was a way that I could live like that. I wanted to know him, to learn from

*him, to get underneath his skin. And I also thought that he might be
the key to my winning over the charming and beautiful Eva Ní Riain.*

The camera pans slowly away from the flashing lights in
the train window to Miles again, and he begins to move. He
manages to drag himself up to a sitting position, then to pull
himself up on to the train seat where he lies flat on his back.

'I'm sorry about that,' he says to the ceiling, speaking in
a woozy way as if he is drunk, 'I didn't mean to scare you.
I'll be fine in a while, just need to have a bit of a sleep.'

'I'll get you into a taxi and take you home,' says Hamish.
'My name's Hamish by the way. Hamish McGrath.'

'One of our bookkeepers is called that.'

'That's me. Assistant Chief.'

'You can count on Hamish McGrath.'

'That's right. You can count on me, don't worry.'

And here the camera surprises us by pulling back away
from the scene in the carriage and backwards out of the
train window and we see the train is on a high-level approach
into the city, with the lit-up tall office blocks and hotels of
Birmingham all around it. We watch it go, with Miles and
Hamish inside, until it eventually disappears underground
into New Street Station and the camera lingers on the city
for a while, as if it is this huge city we should be interested
in not those hopeless people and their puny, pointless lives.

The characters in film noir often feel smaller than the
places they inhabit – especially here in *Out of the Dark*. High-
rise buildings loom over everything. The massive machines
in the car factory seem to control the workers rather than
vice versa. Wide motorways slice through the city centre
high above everyone's heads, sending pedestrians diving
deep down into dark underpasses. *Out of the Dark* gives a
sense that Birmingham's city centre has no geographical

meaning to its inhabitants, that each small area, such as a shopping mall, or a church, or a car park, is not linked to the next. There is no human or emotional scale to the way people move around in Birmingham city centre, people are in one place and then suddenly in another, and everything is linked up by damp-looking, beige-walled tunnels and wind-blasted high-level pedestrian bridges. It was as if the spaces between were unimportant, or didn't actually exist. *Out of the Dark* made Birmingham itself seem like a film – as if all its individual places had been shot in entirely different locations and then stitched together to form an imaginary whole.

I paused the tape there and sat and thought about the relationship between Miles and Hamish. It was all there in the difference between their names. Hamish, the name so solid and trustworthy, but also comical somehow. And old, as if he could be from another century. And then the name Miles, the implications of a long way travelled, a hidden depth, or just the sheer insinuation of a large size. Hamish seemed like an indoor name and Miles was outdoor.

I thought about the names of all the other characters I had encountered so far and listed them in my head. But none of these names seemed to be the right one.

I went out on to the balcony and sat on my specially rigged-up seat to watch the cars and vans climbing up the slip road and merging. The way the underpasses and over-passes looped around each other made me think of the tubes and wires in the hospital linking the bodies up to the machines.

I stiffened when I saw a dark BMW pull up outside the flat. A tall, thin man in black suit trousers and a heavy-look-ing padded coat got out and stood next to the car. He made a blade of his hand to shield his eyes against the winter sun and looked up towards my flat.

Fiona's dad.

I ducked down and hid on the floor.

How had he found me?

Fiona's dad walked to the door of the flats and I heard the rasp of a buzzer going off in a flat not far away.

I didn't move.

He wasn't dangerous. But he must be in a state. I couldn't meet him at this moment. I just couldn't. I wasn't fit for human consumption. I suspected that, deep down, Fiona's father, Melvin, disliked me anyway, despite what had happened. We had nothing in common and it riled him that I did no work other than write about one certain film every now and again for obscure journals. Melvin was an accountant at an estate agent's. He could count things. He could count houses. He could count the money it took to buy houses and the money it cost to take photographs of them and the money it cost to show people round them. He was practical. In many ways he was very like Hamish in *Out of the Dark*. He voted Conservative and didn't believe in anything lefty or alternative or arty and he always ignored all the talk about my ambitions to be a full-time film studies academic, instead continually bringing back news of Daniel Quinn-shaped vacancies at the estate agent's. I had to spend a lot of time thinking of excuses not to apply for those positions. Now, I could hear that low, soft voice with the small high-pitched crack in it, as he called out loudly through the intercom into another flat he had rung.

Maybe he hadn't come looking for me at all. Maybe it was a coincidence. Maybe someone wanted to purchase their flat – right-to-buy was all the rage – and he was coming round to look at the finances. That was the sort of thing Melvin did.

'Sorry, wrong address, mate,' I heard out of the crackly speaker, and then I peeped out over the balcony and saw him go back to his car. He leaned on it for a few minutes while he looked at the two blocks of flats. He took a piece of paper from out of his pocket, unfolded it, looked at it carefully, then put it away. He looked at the grassy area and watched a group of teenagers wander across it leaving a trail of mess behind them and bashing each other's heads with rolled-up school exercise books as they went down towards the defunct arcade of shops.

After Melvin had gone I put on my denim jacket and went out. I was going to have to spend time out of the flat more often if they now knew where I was.

I decided to go for a long walk, into Walsall town centre, back to the pub where I'd had what might be called my first date with Fiona.

The Wheatsheaf looked exactly the same as it had back then. Still divided into three rooms – a bar, a lounge and a snug – and the red banquette velveteen seating looked the same as well. It was nearly empty so I was able to find the exact seat I had sat in that night, and I sat there and drank a Guinness while I pieced together the events of that night one year and seven months ago.

CHAPTER EIGHT

1986

The pub walls were painted a dark yellow colour, not quite dark enough to be brown, but giving the effect of brown. They were the same colour back then. There also used to be a jukebox full of records but this had been replaced by a quiz machine. On the end of the bar, where there was once a jar of hard-boiled eggs floating in dark brown vinegar, bags of pork scratchings sat in a basket.

When she entered the room my skin had begun to tingle. It was as if a film star had stepped off the screen and entered real life. She wasn't wearing her silver stage clothes, or her fancy high shoes, or her hat; but she had a presence, a presence that made everyone in the bar stop what they were doing and look at her. She was tall and thin like some Scandinavian goddess and because on that particular evening she didn't have a hat on, I realised for the first time that her head was completely shaved down to the skin.

She spotted me in the corner and came over and sat down opposite me without saying anything. I rose up quickly and was about to ask her what she wanted to drink when her head bobbed towards the door and she called out, 'Hey, good timing you lot, we're over here,' and the rest of the band, the quiet mousy guitar-vocalist girl and the maths-geek synth man, tumbled through the door in a rush, as if someone was pushing them out of a burning van.

The quiet girl sat next to me and the maths fella sat opposite, next to the dancer. At this time I didn't know her name and she wasn't forthcoming with it. I looked at her legs, long and smooth, stretched out so far that her equally long foot was nearly touching mine. She was wearing green spangly leggings with purple leg warmers and high-top New Balance trainers on her feet.

I was not tall and I was wondering how sex would work between a short man and a tall woman.

The white-spectacled maths guy stared at me with a frown, then said, 'So. You getting the drinks in? If you want us to play at your musical recital concert you'll have to puffle us a bit, won't you?'

They all laughed and I joined in, but then, as if in choreographed unison, the trio's laughter stopped abruptly, and my own laughter went on, sounding shrill and false as it bounced off the dark yellow walls.

They stared at me for a long time.

'We have to be able to trust you,' the maths man said. 'Can we trust you?'

'You can.'

'Prove it.'

'I can't.'

'Sell us some drugs.'

'I don't have any drugs.'

'People who don't know how to buy drugs don't know how to buy records. And people who don't know how to buy records don't know how to put on festivals.'

'What about I buy you a drink?' I said.

'OK,' he said and looked at the others.

'Three double whiskies, please,' the tall dancer said, 'and three pints of Grolsch.'

I pretended I wasn't surprised at their audacious order and went to the bar to place it, knowing that this bill would bite a huge chunk out of my weekly giro. But it was worth it for this fabulous woman, who was clearly interested in me if she had bothered to show up, despite bringing her annoying friends along. Maybe she was not as confident as she seemed and brought them along for support.

As I placed the drinks in front of them, I asked them what they were all called.

'I'm the dancer,' she said.

'I'm synthesisers,' maths man said.

'And I'm guitar and vocals,' the quiet mousy one said, smiling at me in a warm and friendly way. 'And occasional synth.'

'Is that like an occasional table?' I asked, but no one laughed.

'One… two… three…' the maths fella said as if counting in a song, then they downed the whiskies and set to on the pints, which they also downed in one.

They looked at the empty glasses.

'Same again?' I said.

'Was the theremin invented in 1920?' the maths guy drawled.

I assumed it was, and I brought the threesome a second lot of drinks and then maths man said, 'You don't mind if we have a quick band meeting before we talk about your festival, do you?'

'Of course not,' I said. 'Go ahead.' And I took a sip of my Guinness.

'It would need to be in private,' the dancer said.

'Oh,' I said, 'OK.'

And I went off and into the back room. Before sitting down I went back and shoved my head through the door.

'How will I know when −'

'You'll know,' the dancer said.

'OK,' I said.

In the snug an old man was drinking a half of stout and reading the *Racing Post*. He was tiny, with white hair and very white skin with grey flecks of beard coming up out of it, and he wore a long dark coat that touched the floor. By his feet was a Merry Hill Centre bag full of empty glass bottles, most of which seemed to have held lemonade.

I sat down opposite him.

'Cold out, isn't it?' the man said.

'Yes,' I said.

The man's trousers were made of soft cloth like pyjamas and I wondered whether he had escaped from a hospital and stolen the coat from a doctor.

'I'm going to go into West Brom in a while. I like it better than Walsall. Smaller, more friendly. There's a café there where you can get a pensioner's all-day breakfast for 90p and then I'm getting my hair cut and then I'm meeting a mate at the betting shop. Then we are going to the pub. It's changed so much, though, West Bromwich. Once I used to know everyone and now it's all strangers.'

I sensed a racist comment in the wind and headed it off.

'It's good that people around here are so welcoming. They welcome everyone who wants to come and live in the area, don't they? All types, wherever they are from.'

'Yes,' the old man said, somewhat reluctantly. 'But you can be too kind for your own sake, can't you?'

I looked towards the door and strained to see if I could hear the members of Pop Pop Pop! discussing their future plans for the electronic trio but nothing carried through the thick pub walls.

I had another pint of Guinness, and bought the old man a half as well, and he told me all about his granddaughter who was on a gap year, temping in Australia.

'She's working on a rail crash enquiry, transcribing witness statements. She doesn't get to go to the hearings, but it's interesting. She sends me letters about it. Well, sends her mother letters, and her mother tells me what they say. When something goes wrong, when a plane crashes or when a building explodes, we analyse everything that happened before the incident – in great detail – don't we? To try and learn from it. Try and work out what went wrong, so that we don't repeat the mistakes. It makes sense. But why don't we do the same when things go well? If we looked at something that went well in as much detail, we might be able to repeat it. Like winning the World Cup in 1966. Or putting up the Empire State Building.'

'The problem is,' I said, 'people can't agree on what went well. Some people don't like modern buildings, like the Empire State Building.'

But the old man wouldn't give up on this theory. 'We need to learn from our achievements as well as our mistakes,' he kept saying, and gave me several more examples of great achievements, including the British Empire and the invention of zips.

After my third pint with the old man, an hour and a half had passed since my exile to the snug. No one had come to find me or update me, so I decided I would see what was going on.

I put my head around the door to discover that my date had gone and so had logarithm boy.

The jukebox was playing 'Holiday' by Madonna, and the barman was staring at a big clock while shuffling a tower of beer mats.

The room was empty.

Except for the mousy guitarist (and occasional synth) who was sitting in the corner reading a book.

'They had to go and see someone about a PA for next week,' she called over.

I sat down next to her. Her spectacles were so far down her nose they looked to be falling off. Behind them she had dark brown eyes that looked wet, like a recently mopped marble floor. Her hair was black, and shiny like moleskin, and her spectacles were black-rimmed like Nana Mouskouri's.

The book she was reading was a large hardback called *The New Music – Berg, Messiaen, Schoenberg, Stockhausen and Others*.

'I just got a place at the conservatoire in Birmingham,' she said, 'hence the nerd book. I'll be starting a PhD in composition and free improvisation.'

She spoke very quietly so I had to lean right next to her to hear what she said, and she had a habit of laughing at the end of every sentence, inflating each last word with a bubble of humour.

'Let me get you a drink. It's not fair that you had to get that great big round in.'

I looked at her plain brogue-ish shoes and red and white stripy socks, her baggy stone-washed dungarees and her black specs and her dull-looking book and thought, oh my God, I'll never find anything to talk to this girl about for the length of one whole drink, and I was worried I wouldn't be able to drink my Guinness fast enough.

Five drinks later Fiona and I were outside and she was showing me the bus timetable and explaining how I could, if I wanted, get on the famous number 11 and go all the way round the city, over and over.

'Like Hamish says in *Out of the Dark*.'

'Yes,' she said, and laughed as if I had made a great joke, but I could see she hadn't heard of the film.

'One of these days,' she said, 'I am going to turn a bus timetable into a piece of music. It'll be very easy. I will relate certain notes, rests, silences and beats with certain bus numbers and bus stops and it will write itself. I'm off now – I live over there in the Chuckery. Go back inside. I don't want you to watch me go. I will feel myself shrinking on the surface of your eyeballs, becoming a little tiny dot.'

I went back inside and stood in the corridor, to give her time to get out of sight. The old man came out of the snug and stopped next to me.

'Must have been a good meeting,' he said.

'Very good,' I said. 'Might have been the best meeting I've ever had in my life.'

'You should analyse why it was good,' he said. 'Like I was saying earlier. Analyse everything that you did to make that meeting happen and then you can keep repeating those things throughout the rest of your life,' and he went off towards the bus stop, his large coat trailing on the floor making him look as though he was gliding along.

'Kid' by the Pretenders came on the jukebox and I listened to it carefully, as if for some reason it might be important. The band play the song very fast yet it leaves the impression in your mind of a slow emotional ballad. Maybe this was what I should learn from the evening, even though I had no idea what it might mean at all.

I never saw the dancer again and Fiona left Pop Pop Pop! a week later, after an argument about a complicated time signature that logarithm man was unable to program into his drum machine.

CHAPTER NINE

1988

Almost as soon as I had taken off my jacket the buzzer went
and it was John Ireland.

'Come up,' I said and pressed the door release.

He used the stairs, and as I was on the seventh floor, it
was a few minutes later when he arrived. I was surprised to
see that he wasn't at all out of breath because to get there in
that time he must have bounded up two at a time.

'Have you made up your mind?'

'What about?' I said.

'Renting me your garage.'

'Oh. Yes,' I said. 'You can have the garage.'

'Great,' he said. 'Did you get my draft contract?'

He was referring, I guessed, to the slip of paper he'd put
through my door.

'I'm not sure about signing that,' I said.

'How about a gentlemen's agreement then?'

'That would be fine.'

I invited him into the hall and when he got inside he
stopped still and stared all about him – at the floor, at the
walls, through the open doors of the kitchen and the living

room, and even up at the ceiling, all the while with a look of fascination on his face as if he was inside a mysterious painted cave that had never before been seen by man.

'You don't have much stuff,' he said, finally.

'No,' I said.

'I like that,' he said. 'You can really breathe.'

He brought out a cheque book and a small stubby ballpoint pen, wrote me a cheque for the amount we had agreed, and held it out to me.

But before I took it from him I said, 'There's one condition.'

'What's that?' he asked, yanking his hand away as if I was about to set his cheque on fire.

'I'd like to know why you want to own all the garages and what you keep in them.'

'Then the deal is off,' he said, and he lifted the cheque up in front of my face and tore it in two, very, very slowly, an expression of intense concentration on his face, as if he was listening carefully to the tearing sound it made. Then he stuffed the two halves into his pocket and walked out.

I went to the balcony and after a while saw him emerge from the main door and disappear over the grassy area. I knew he would enter the Frog and Railway and sit on his own at the end of the bar, scowling into his beer, because I had seen him through the window in the same position when I passed the pub on my way to the bus stop.

I sat down on the chair that I had balanced on the stool and settled to watch the traffic.

I felt worn out.

The traffic was flowing quickly and cars and vans were dancing in and out of the lanes as they changed their routes and switched motorways. I wondered why there weren't more crashes, and thought about all those thousands of tons of metal thundering along on curved ribbons of concrete in the air, and wondered why it wasn't a horrifying sight. It ought to be a disturbing vision of hell, it ought to be the worst thing you could ever see. Yet its beauty was something that calmed me and made me think not of the violence of the combustion engines exploding over and over and the reckless speeds of the vehicles but of the potential of human beings – how we are able to design things, and build things, and cooperate, and achieve enormous tasks outside of any of our individual capabilities – the cars and the roads and the rules and the systems which make everything work together.

I went back inside and sat in front of the video player and pressed play. My search must continue.

At this point in the film there was an abrupt cut to a modern high-rise flat looking out over a huge panorama of Birmingham. I examined it carefully to see whether this scene had also been filmed here on the Yew Tree Estate, but no. It was much higher up, probably the top of a twenty-one-floor block – there were many of these in Birmingham. From the flat in the film you could see the Rotunda in the city centre, planes moving through the sky almost at the same height as the flat, and in the distance, the dim outlines of the Worcestershire and Malvern Hills.

In the flat sit Hamish and Miles's wife, Mrs Dawson.

An elegantly curved blond coffee table (G Plan, I guessed, as the film's credits had foretold) is covered with glossy books about houses and gardens. Everything is very formal and very sixties. Nibbles in bowls, and drinks in tiny glasses.

Miles's wife is prim and tidy and housewifely in her manner. She is often seen in the film wearing a housecoat and carrying dusters and cloths and is deliberately non-sexual compared to Eva. However, she is played by Patricia O'Shea, who would be seen later in the sixties as a fly-by-night good-time girl in the sitcom *Steptoe and Son*, when she is brought home by the young Harold Steptoe after a night out, Harold's bid to seduce her being thwarted by his dad's obnoxious unhygienic habits. Some of her overt sexuality does slip through in this role, though, particularly in this scene in the way she drinks her tea and nibbles a long wafer, but you can see she is trying her best to play a full-on frump.

Hamish tells her all about meeting Miles and how he had the fit and the misunderstanding about the bag. Miles is asleep all this time in his bed.

'He can sleep for hours after a seizure. A long, long time,' Mrs Dawson tells Hamish. 'You say you also work at the plant?'

'Bean-counter. My people and Miles's people are usually at odds, to be honest.'

'Oh yes. The cuts.'

'The proposals for role-sharing on the line.'

'Mister-in-there calls every change a cut. An attack on the working man's dignity.'

'It's all in Miles's hands really. Miles has the negotiating power. It's a closed shop.'

'He likes to be in control.'

'Are you happy together?' Hamish says.

'Of course,' she says. 'Yes. Why do you ask?'

'Oh, I ask everyone,' says Hamish. 'When I am away on business or out on my own with colleagues, *my* wife, Florence, she worries. She gets very jealous. Don't you ever get jealous, Mrs Dawson? Don't you wonder where Miles is after work? What with all these late union meetings?'

'I trust him, Mr −?'

'McGrath. But call me Hamish.'

'I trust him, Hamish McGrath. I trust him implicitly. Look.'

She gets up and goes to the window and he follows and they stand next to each other and gaze out over the city, with their backs to the camera.

'There are a lot of people in this city – nearly half a million – and a lot of things go on. If I had a magic eye and could zoom in on all those windows in all those flats and houses, what do you think I might see?'

'I don't know.'

The camera swoops over their heads and somehow travels through the glass, as it did earlier in the restaurant, and then, as she speaks, it hovers over the city like a guardian angel looking down on everything.

'Do you think I would see things I want to see? No. I would see things I don't want to see. Without a doubt. So I trust him. I don't want to be a magic eye, X-raying and surveying the city, watching my husband all day long. When Miles walks out of this scene, he isn't around any more. But he is always in here.'

Cut back to inside the flat, to a head-and-shoulders shot of Miles's wife tapping her hand where her heart would be. 'He is in here all of the time.'

She sits down again and leaves Hamish standing there looking out of the window, rubbing his chin. Penderecki's music seeps in here, almost surreptitiously, two high-pitched discordant violin notes, followed by a deep cello note that falls and falls and keeps falling as if it is descending into the underworld. At this point in the film Hamish's stifled emotions and buried secret desires seem to endow his every gesture and facial expression with an operatic passion.

Then we see Hamish leaving the flat and as he does so there is a close-up of him taking the folded drawing from out of his pocket, looking at it, then replacing it.

Cut to Hamish at home, reading a book called *Industrial Relations: Theory and Practice.*

Florence, his wife, is watching the television. Florence is played by Maureen Fleming, who previously played a farmer's wife in Radio 4 soap *The Archers*. She looks like a stereotyped sixties housewife, forever in a pinny, a worried little pinched mouth, slippers on her feet, teapot ever poised over a cup and saucer. There is a definite visual and cultural rhyme with Miles's wife as if the film is saying all wives either are the same, or become the same. Tonight she is watching *Sunday Night at the London Palladium* and laughing her head off. Hamish looks at her mouth wide open and as she laughs the laughing becomes distorted and the camera goes towards the mouth, getting so close so that it fills the screen. It's an awkward effect, very over the top, but in this instance works to justify Hamish's mood of desperation, and of being trapped in a domestic nightmare. The camera flips to her point of view of him and he gets up and tosses the book down on the coffee table.

'I'm tired. I'm going to have a lie-down,' he says.

'Bruce Forsyth is making this woman look like such a fool,' she says.

'I'm going up. Did you hear me?'

'OK, sugar,' she says. 'There's no need to shout. It's only half past nine, you know.'

'I have an important paper to present tomorrow. For the management team. About protected jobs. Changing people's roles on the line, asking them to vary the jobs they do.

But you know how rigid that union is. Demarcation, differentials.'

'You won't get anything past that Miles Dawson.'

'You heard of Dawson?'

'He's always in the news whenever there's trouble at your place.'

'I don't watch the local news.'

'You should, because it's about you and me and people round here.'

'I prefer to hear about people from other places.'

'They say he runs rings round the bosses.'

'I can handle Miles Dawson, don't you worry,' he says, and the camera cuts to Florence, staring at him with a doubting smile on her lips.

'Whatever you say, darling,' she adds, and turns back to watching *Beat the Clock*.

I paused the tape.

I liked the way Schneider, the director, was racking up the sexual tension, making Hamish appear useless and small compared to the heroic Miles Dawson. Giving Miles epilepsy elevates him in some way, making him a holy innocent – godlike, almost. At this time in the sixties epilepsy was not that well understood and it is fascinating that Otto Schneider chose to include this aspect in the film at all.

I found a piece of paper and began to write down the names of all the characters in the film. Once I had the list I began to make anagrams out of the names to see if that helped.

Nothing worked, nothing was coming out of this exercise at all so far.

I went for a long walk around the Yew Tree, running all the names through my head, testing them, weighing them to see if any of them felt right. I walked a couple of miles all the way into Walsall centre then I went up the hill to Caldmore Green where Fiona and I used to live when we first got together.

Number 45.

I stood outside the house and looked in through the window.

The downstairs front room was no longer a bedroom. A family was living there, judging from the toys, small bikes and clutter I could see in the hall through the glass door. The upstairs curtains moved and I saw the shape of someone behind the glass. They must have been wondering why I was standing on the pavement opposite and looking in.

CHAPTER TEN

1986

Fiona and I met up or spoke to each other on the phone every day after that night in the Wheatsheaf. Whenever we were together or on the phone there was never an uncomfortable silence between us, never an awkwardness. If there was silence, it was the good kind, the kind that settles about you like snow and you both watch it covering everything and changing the shape of the things you just said and the things you were about to say.

I was living at the time in a shared house with two blokes, Brian and Simon. But as it was the summer holidays they had gone back home, so the house was empty. It was a two-bed terraced house on a street in Caldmore, in the centre of Walsall, and had been furnished cheaply from the local second-hand shops. Just the minimum. No bedside tables, or footstools, or table lamps. When we decided we needed a coffee table we bought a dining table and sawed off the legs. As you can imagine, a coffee table of that size gathered a lot of fly-tipped detritus from three untidy blokes. The day after Brian and Simon went away for the summer I bought a big old television and placed it on a plastic bucket. As everyone from college, including the staff, had deserted the town for the holidays, I imagined that watching TV would be my only entertainment. That is, until I met Fiona. After that, of course, everything revolved about her, or rather me and her. And we never mentioned the glamorous dancer who had been my first attraction. Fiona was a local, from West Bromwich, and she, like me, was a so-called mature student, i.e. we hadn't got into college through the traditional route of studying hard and getting good A levels. We were twenty-five. Both of us were twenty-five, and we liked being twenty-five. And we liked the fact that both of us had ignored A levels and pursued other goals. Fiona had concentrated on her band, and me, well I had concentrated on playing pool in the pub and watching old films. I was excited by Fiona not just because she was Fiona, and clever and pretty and all of that, but also because she was from a city. A big city, where she grew up. Cities were where everyone else came from, people who you heard about in the newspapers and on the television. Cities were where everything happened. You would never be alone in a city, I thought. Cities were where film noirs happened and I think at that age I actually wanted to be in a film noir. I felt that if you were in a city all you had to do was go out of your house and find a bar and then buy a drink and sit and wait. Then, almost definitely, something would happen to you. You would meet a woman with a complicated life who would, without pause, begin to involve you in it. The bar staff would become your friends and enlist you into all kinds of thrilling late-night activities. Men would appear in the bar and ask you to help them with jobs which may or may not be illegal. There would be drugs. I saw myself in all of this as the kind of cerebral intellectual type, always on the fringes of a gang, the one who works out the complicated maths and logistics for a bank job, and who the real gangsters call *the professor* and pat on the back while rolling their eyes. But in the end the glamorous blonde in the group, the one who the lead gangster would smack about now and again, actually had her eye on me. This was the fantasy world I lived in during my late teens in the backwaters of west Cumbria.

Fiona and I settled into a rhythm. My bedroom was downstairs, in the former front room, and Fiona would stay over with me when she could. On many occasions we spent the whole day in bed, having sex, drinking coffee, and eating cheese on toast. We put the fan heater on when it was cold. We had a small portable cassette player and I had a few cassettes, and she brought round mix tapes of music I hadn't heard. Often we lay together while the Cocteau Twins washed about us, or Red Guitars, or some other new band I didn't know. She also played me the modern composers she studied for her course – Philip Glass, and Stockhausen and John Cage, and I loved all of it.

She had broad musical taste, and also liked an album by Ella Fitzgerald – *Hits From The American Song Book* or something like that – and we lay for hours listening to that album over and over, laughing at the funny rhymes, like the fish that grin from fin to fin. But in reality we were overcome with the powerful feelings of loss and yearning that throbbed from within those ballads from the forties. To me, if I closed my eyes I could imagine the music being performed by a small fragile-looking woman wearing furs and feathers in a dark jazz club late at night that we had spilled into accidentally through an unmarked door. Accompanying the singer would be a worried-looking piano player who had money problems and a drug habit and was paid in beer.

A few men would be talking business at a long bar. There would be couples scattered about, mainly older men with very young women who they were trying to impress, and the bar manager would be a loud mustachioed smoothie in a white suit who walked about and shook everyone's hand and asked if they were having a good time and, with a wink, did they need anything else?

Fiona and I would stick out a mile in this club, me in my black denim jacket and black jeans and Dr. Martens boots, and Fiona in Sophia Loren specs, short skirt, black tights and astrakhan jacket from the rag market. Everyone would say, 'Hey, you two, how did you end up in here?', and laugh, and buy us drinks. Gimlets, we would drink gimlets. We would stare at the singer while nodding our heads. We would look with intelligent and knowledgeable appreciation at the piano player's hands as they moved up and down the keyboard. We would be infiltrators in another world and we would love it.

In a few weeks she would be starting her Master's at the Birmingham conservatoire – composition and free improvisation. Did I mind if she came round to mine and did some work there? Of course not, I said. And so she would spread her papers out on the floor and 'make some work'. She would have her guitar and a little Casio keyboard and a four-track tape machine and I would sit and watch, enthralled as she fabricated noises and tunes and textures and moods, hardly any of which I would have described as music, but all of which I loved for the ambition and the risk and the danger of it all. I liked the fact that behind everything she composed there was some kind of system. For example, maybe every other note would last for one beat longer than the last, or maybe there was a secret numbering system that informed every chord change or maybe there was something based on the fractal patterns in the way a fern grows.

Music charts and scores and text books and bits of paper covered in dots and diagrams were all over the place and although I didn't understand any of it, I loved that it was everywhere like this; it was like being drowned in a sea of her intellect and her emotion, and I wanted to allow it to cover me. The more impenetrable her descriptions of her work became, the more I loved it. Of one piece she said: 'Think of it as though we are moving through a Pythagorean curtain of sound.' She explained her composing like this: 'Most rock music works horizontally – there is a drum line then a bass line layered on top of that, then riffs and melodies on top of those, and that's how the music moves along.' She made a shape with her hand like a swimming fish. 'Like, say, *Tubular Bells* or Pink Floyd or Jean-Michel Jarre. But what I do is entirely vertical. Each bar of music can be completely different to the last one, and that's why it takes so long.' Her hand changed to an upright blade that moved through the air in staccato jumps. 'It's forensic, and detailed, and completely absorbing.' Then she told me about her forthcoming performance at the conservatoire in which she intended to use a 1920s mechanical zither recorded on to a wax cylinder, a rhythm machine made of Meccano cogs, a pile of shredded paper stirred by an electric fan, and a circular system of prepared flutes.

It was when she asked me to help her to write the submission cover note that had to go in with her assignment that I had to tell her about my reading and writing issues – and I wasn't surprised when she told me she suffered from some of the same problems.

'Words to me are a big swirling mess,' she said. 'That's why I love maths and music.'

We realised that our minds worked differently to everyone else's. For example, neither of us had understood figures of speech when we were younger. Fiona told me how she had got upset when she heard the term *did he fall or was he pushed* about her uncle losing his job, thinking he'd been hurt in some way. And I told her about my father calling a big banking company *a stumbling giant* and how I kept thinking about this poor gigantic man in the bank stumbling about because he was blind, or disabled in some way.

During that first summer she showed me the sights of Birmingham. All the places she used to go to in her youth. Barbarella's where she saw Blondie and Elvis Costello. The Odeon where she was watching *Planet of the Apes* when the IRA bomb went off in the Mulberry Bush next door. The Silver Blades ice rink on Pershore Road where her dad used to take her ice dancing. Her old school, out in the suburbs in Weoley Castle. The Sandwell Valley park in West Bromwich, next to the motorway. I liked the park best precisely because it was next to the motorway. My love of all the grit and dirt of the urban scene was one thing Fiona didn't understand about me.

'What, you mean the Lake District?' she said when I told her I was from west Cumbria. Even though I lived in it, the Lake District was another world. A world where visitors with multi-pocketed trousers and maps in plastic bags around their necks chose to walk to the top of high, misty hills, where I assumed there was nothing to see but more high, misty hills, regimented rows of pine trees, and sheep, sheep, sheep, sheep, sheep. It turned out that Fiona knew the hills and mountains better than my friends and family in Cumbria and she promised to take me walking up the fells when we went up there. She had maps, boots, waterproofs, everything.

I pretended I was interested, but I wasn't really. The day with Fiona I remember best was the time we took the number 11 bus and rode it all day around Birmingham, recreating the scene from *Out of the Dark*, when the protagonist Hamish is so scared it's the only place he can think of hiding. It may well have been true that I knew nothing about the so-called beautiful fells that were a few miles from my parents' house, but it turned out that Fiona knew nothing about *Out of the Dark* – the sixties film noir that had been filmed in her own city – and I spent a long time explaining it to her, including all the local settings.

One night we watched it together.

I could speak along with every word of it if needs be, but I refrained from doing so. What I did was watch Fiona's face and body language as she experienced it and at the end I couldn't wait to find out what she thought. I was relieved. She liked it. She didn't love it in the way I did, but she loved the fact that it was filmed and set in Birmingham and it was a film noir from England.

We talked a little about the way women were usually portrayed in film noirs – as femme fatales, as crazy, untrustworthy loons, as power-hungry monsters who used sex as a weapon. But strangely she wasn't horrified by the way the women were used in these pictures – more by the ways the films portrayed men. 'Why are they all so weak?' she said. 'I mean, it's as if they would do anything – and I mean anything – all the way from robbery to kidnap to murder – just for the chance of a few hours between the sheets with a hot bitch like Eva Ni Riain? I mean, would you steal a car or kill a man to sleep with someone like her?' she had asked me. 'Well, would you?'

It was a good question. In truth, I didn't know, and it was something I wondered about a lot. What would I do for Fiona, for example? Would I do anything? Sometimes I thought that was the case.

I suggested watching the film again right away but she didn't jump at the chance; instead she wanted to talk to me about the composer, Penderecki. As it happened, Penderecki was a composer she would be studying at the conservatoire when she started her course in September, and she was surprised that he was part of such a low-budget affair. It was before his music had been used in *The Shining* and *The Exorcist*, I explained. And he was never properly credited for *Out of the Dark*. In fact, he took his name off the film because he said he wasn't proud of the work. He felt that his music for *Out of the Dark* was too obvious, too emotionally guiding. It ended up being credited to a name that was always used in the film industry when someone on a film didn't want their contribution to be known: Alan Smithee. However, Fiona loved the soundtrack, and what she wanted to do was listen to the whole soundtrack again without the images. For her, that was the real deal. So I worked out a way of getting the whole soundtrack, all one hour twenty-seven minutes of it, on to a tape, and the next time we were in my bedroom, I put it on. From then on that became our track of choice for lazing about in bed and having sex. There is something about dialogue and movie scenes mixed with heady music when listened to without the pictures which makes them a whole different art form all together. It becomes abstract, and although you wouldn't think it, you can listen to it over and over. Enjoy the musicality of the way the actors talk, the way their words become just sounds, and the rhythms and inflections of everything in the film stick in your head like a symphony. Fiona had introduced me to a new way of enjoying my favourite film and sometimes, when she wasn't in and I was reading, or cooking, or having a bath, or just lying around, I would put on the soundtrack and it made an excellent aural bed for all kinds of thinking and planning and ruminating.

When she started the course that September, she would come back to the house bursting with stories about the other students and the lecturers, bouncing on her toes with excitement as she moved about the room. By now I had met her parents too. Her mother was a lovely, tall lady who had been a dancer on cruise ships and in nightclubs, and had met her father when he was a drummer in a house band. There had been a big fire in the Isle of Man holiday camp where they were performing, and the story goes that he rescued her from the flames by smashing through a door and carrying her down a smoke-choked flight of stairs. All around the house there were black and white pictures of her in towering stilettos, high-kicking in a row of girls with feathers on their heads and sparkly leotards, and in some of them you could make out her father at the back, sweating on a kit of Ludwig drums with the name of the big band on the skin of the bass. Nowadays her mother ran a dance school at weekends and her father counted the money for Firth, Wesser and Holden, property consultants, in Harborne.

Fiona moved into mine a few weeks after we met and eventually we rented a whole house to ourselves near a factory with a smoking chimney in the Chuckery area of Walsall.

That was where we stayed until the following summer.

Last summer.

CHAPTER ELEVEN

1988

Betty rattled the letterbox at 8.30 that evening.

'Navigator?' she said.

'Compliance,' I said.

Agnes was sitting in her kitchen looking out of the window towards the garages. She was dressed in proper clothes for a change – neat, slim jeans, high-heeled shoes and a baggy jumper as big as a coat. She was still wearing the shades though, along with the furry beret.

'Sit with me for a time would you, Quinn. I sometimes feel so desperate, so unhappy, and all I want is to have someone sit next to me. But please don't speak or ask me anything. Please just sit.'

I sat down on the sofa with her, facing the window. She was smoking as usual and drinking something white and chemical-smelling.

We looked at the garages and she was staring so intently it looked as though she was expecting something to happen.

Nothing did.

A woman with a pushchair and a large white smooth-haired dog came into view and when she came to the garages she slowed down and stared at them as if, even for her, they held some sort of mystery.

Then a council van parked up next to the garages and a man got out and examined a lamppost. He wrote something on to a clipboard, got back into his van, and drove away. He didn't even look over at the garages, even though they did in fact belong to the council, not John Ireland. Over on the grassy area some teenaged boys walked over to the phone box where they were always hanging around.

Agnes and I sat like that for an hour or so, neither of us saying anything. I found it relaxing, like sitting with a cat.

Eventually, she sighed and shifted her position.

'I miss my real place,' she said. 'In Paris. Beautiful flat on Rue Daguerre in Montparnasse. The street cafés, the little cheese stalls, the fishmongers and butchers, the jazz club, the scooters tearing up and down, the old men sitting outside with espressos reading *Paris Match*. The bakers – wonderful fresh bread, you can't get it here – the tiny old cinema showing old American crime films. The Montparnasse cemetery where Jean-Paul Sartre and Samuel Beckett and Serge Gainsbourg are buried. You should see all the flowers and cards and gifts on Gainsbourg's grave. The whole of France loved him. But on Beckett's grave, nothing. As an atheist and existentialist he insisted that nothing be put there to commemorate him, and the public respect this. One day you will come.'

'I've never been abroad,' I said. 'Never felt the need. Is it worth it?'

'Paris is not abroad. Paris is the capital of everywhere.'

We fell silent again and stared at the black painted doors of the garages. They looked like a row of dark portals to somewhere else.

'The way he talks about them,' she said, after some time. '*The garages*, he always says. Like that. *The garages*, and his eyes go watery. It's as if he goes off to another place in his head entirely.'

She tapped out another cigarette, lit it, and took a long pull.

'I like him, Quinn, I like John Ireland. I like his innocence. He is not like any other man I've ever known. He is like an obsessive child who collects random things for no reason. A bird that collects scraps of tin it has no use for. It seems to me that for John Ireland the garages are something else – not garages at all, but a different category of things. It's as if he is an alien with different perceptions. Maybe for him the garages have a completely different shape, or colour, or feel, or smell. Maybe they make a sound that only he can hear. Maybe it's like those people who can hear colours or see smells. Maybe the garages give off a vibration which only he can sense. Or maybe they even have a different dimension. In any case, why would a big handsome bloke like that with a job and a family want to bother himself with owning random scruffy garages that even he never visits.'

'I guess it's a case of each to their own,' I said.

She looked at me with contempt when I said this.

'Anyway,' she said, 'I asked Betty to go to the library and get me some books about local history. And guess what I found out? A number of years ago there was something interesting on the exact site of those garages.'

'Oh.'

'A funeral director's. It was pulled down in the sixties when they put this lot up. And before the funeral director's, it was – guess what?'

I couldn't.

'A brothel. And before the brothel, it belonged to the church. It was an alms house. So religion, then sex, then death, isn't that interesting?'

'I've got to go and finish my work,' I said. 'Sorry.'

'You annoy me, Quinn. What do you do over there, for all the hours that the days hold? You don't seem to go out much. And I never hear any sounds such as music playing or the television. And you have had no visitors since you arrived.'

I raised my eyebrows.

'Betty tells me everything that goes on in these flats. She is my little spy. What is going on, Quinn? No girlfriend? Or boyfriend even? Don't worry, I am broad-minded. You are young!'

'I have a project to finish,' I said. 'It's to do with something that happened to me in Cumbria. I need to find something out and then get back up there as soon as I can.'

I thought back to the hospital, when the doctor had got up off his stool and peered into my eyes.

'Mr Quinn, are you going to be OK?' he had said. And he moved closer to me, and I wanted him to hold me and rock me in his arms.

'I'll tell you all about it,' I said, 'when we have more time,' and I left her gazing out at the garages as if she were looking at an enigmatic painting that became more complicated the more you got to know it.

CHAPTER TWELVE

1988

In film noir, there is always a sense that you are being told a story by a storyteller you can't trust, a version of events from only one person's point of view. In *Out of the Dark*, you will remember that Hamish is telling the story to the police officer down the phone. In many ways, *Out of the Dark* is a very typical film noir in that, not only does it rely on quite a lot of voiceover, but the main story is told in flashback and framed by the teller of the tale, the unreliable narrator, Hamish. So we are at the point in the film now where we cut back from the flashback story to Hamish in the restaurant relating the story to the policeman on the phone, just to remind us that the whole story has ended up with Hamish surrounded by police and holding a woman hostage at gunpoint in a restaurant.

Hamish is talking into the phone.

By the end of that evening I was even more in awe of Miles Dawson. The way he managed to keep his activities with that young floozy completely hidden from his wife was sickening yet somehow enviable. But it was more than that. Now that I knew about the darker side of Miles Dawson, a secret part of me thought I might be able to use this information against him in my negotiations with the union. So I didn't want him to know what I knew. I wanted to lie low. At the same time things were getting close between me and Eva. I was really getting to like her and I believed that she was getting to like me too.

DISSOLVE

The Hollow Egg, where Eva and Hamish are talking.

'Did you get it back? My little instructional diagram?'

'Oh, Eva.' He sighs long and loud. 'No. It would have been a weird thing to ask for.'

'I suppose.'

'Maybe we should observe them. The way a scientist might. See if he stays with the girl or sticks to the wife. It will be an interesting experiment. Might help us decide what we should do.'

'I'm not sure, Hamish.'

'You and I? We are attracted to each other. We both know that. But we are both married to other people. How can we find out what is the right decision to take? We can't. We can never know those things. But this way we can perform an experiment. We can see what happens to those two.'

'But those two are not us.'

'It's the closest we have.'

'You can't treat people like rats in a laboratory.'

'That's the point. They are not rats. They are human. And likely to react to events in the same way as other humans. Like us.'

'Oh, I don't know.'

'You got us into this, Peanut.'

'OK. Let's watch them. See what happens. But I don't think we should interfere or try to change things. Because that just wouldn't be right.'

A period unfolds showing them observing the affair

between Miles and the young woman, from a distance. And as they do so, we see Hamish and Eva touching hands and kissing and we see their affair begin to develop, also. At one point Eva lets her hair down and we see it is actually blonde now, not mousy, and we realise she is the woman from the beginning of the film who Hamish is pointing the gun at. We now wonder how it got from that point to this.

Despite Eva's protestations that they shouldn't intervene, they begin, of course, to do exactly that. They leave little clues for Mrs Dawson and watch her to see what happens. Hamish pops round to see her and Miles every now and then. But whatever Mrs Dawson finds – an earring in Miles's pocket, a receipt for drinks in a cocktail bar – she continues to trust him.

Cut to Hamish and Eva in the pub opposite the young girl's house. By looking at the label on the flat's doorbell they have discovered that the girl is called Miriam. They watch the house and soon find out that Miriam has another boyfriend. They don't see him close up but they see what he is wearing: a distinctive fawn leather jacket and cowboy boots. And they see Miriam saying goodbye to him only minutes before welcoming Dawson inside again.

'I think I know him,' says Eva. 'I recognise that jacket and those boots.'

Cut to the Hollow Egg, and Eva and Hamish looking at a grainy photograph in a newspaper. It is a man standing outside a scruffy pub.

'That's Ronnie Doors, the boxing promoter. See the clothes? No one else wears a leather jacket and boots like that.'

'Is that really him?'

'Definitely, Hamish, it's him. Ronnie Doors himself. He is loaded too.'

'So they are both two-timing?'

'Looks that way. Seems like more people are going to get hurt than we thought.'

'The same as with you and me. If we ever did anything, which we won't.'

'We will.'

'We won't. Listen, I will only agree to be with you properly if this Miles Dawson and Miriam thing works out. If they turn out to really be in love and it works out for the best for them.'

'But how will we know? I've heard of affairs that last a lifetime.'

'Then we should put our foot on the accelerator. Do you have a camera?'

'Yes.'

'Take some happy snaps for Mrs Dawson.'

They begin to kiss, a long lingering one, and the camera pulls away and tracks backwards out of the café. The music rises to a clichéd romantic crescendo, which must have been either an ironic flourish by Penderecki, or a demand from the director which contributed to the composer taking his name off the credits. The camera seems uncertain where to put itself as it dollies backwards to the door, and as the music rises, the camera pans down to the jukebox, then zooms in close on a spinning 45. The record stops revolving, the needle lifts up, and the robotic arm raises the record off the turntable. The title of the song is 'Running Scared' by Roy Orbison.

I was watching, but I wasn't taking it in today. I was becoming too involved with the characters, whereas what I really needed to be doing was looking at the background details and listening to every word to find a clue as to what

Fiona had meant. Also, I was becoming disturbed by sightings of the strange John Ireland hanging around my garage
looking forlorn.

The lift gave out its stink of stale fags and urine and raw
meat. I got in and looked at myself in the mirror and wondered why lifts had mirrors. In film noir, mirrors were a big
feature. People were duplicated and distorted, hinting at
doppelgängers, split personalities, or parallel worlds where
different decisions lead you down completely different paths.

I found John Ireland in the Frog and Railway, sitting on
his favourite high stool, watching, or pretending to watch, a
European football match on a small TV. I sat down next to
him and looked ahead at all the whiskies, gins, brandies and
liqueurs stacked against the mirrored wall.

'Listen,' I said. 'I don't really care why you want to have
all the garages. If it means that much to you, you can have
mine too. You can drop off the cheque tomorrow. Here's
the key.'

He turned slowly to face me and I don't think I have
ever seen a man look so happy. He nearly floated off the
stool. He took the key and gripped it tightly in his fist for a
few moments. Then he shuddered and closed his eyes before
letting out a small, barely audible whimper. It was as though
some uncanny power was being transferred to him from that
object, that small metal object. When he opened his eyes
again they were full of tears and he squeezed my shoulder
and looked me straight in the face.

'Thank you so much,' he said. 'This is not something
that a man like you could ever understand.'

After he had left, I looked at his half-finished pint on the
bar and wondered what he meant by *a man like me*. I didn't
know I was *a man like me*. I never knew what people meant

when they talked about me like that, saying things like *I think you're really going to like this,* or *I don't think this will be your type of thing,* or *you're not really the sort of person we are aiming this at.* This man, this John Ireland, didn't know a thing about me. In fact, I felt that my old self had gone. So what were these vestiges of my old personality that he, this man, this stranger, could see? What were these traces of the previous man who used to inhabit my body?

CHAPTER THIRTEEN

1988

Back in the film it's the next day, and Hamish is in his car using a camera with a long lens to take pictures of Miles with Miriam, his bit of fluff.

Cut to Hamish and Eva standing on a high walkway at the Bull Ring, looking down on the market stalls, whose folded metal awnings look from this high angle like a chemical diagram.

Hamish is showing the pictures to Eva, who nods.

'OK. So are you going to do it or am I?' Hamish says.

Eva takes the handful of six by three photos from him.

'I will put them in the post today,' she says.

The camera lingers on the couple's faces for a time and the two don't say anything, just smile at each other. Then there is a kiss, and the camera pulls focus on their faces, then swoops away, gliding backwards over the market stall awnings before dissolving into a wide crane shot of the Bull Ring from above, with all the shoppers milling around, before finally it pulls back further to reveal that everything is hemmed in by endlessly circling traffic, leaving us with a tableau that resembles a brutal zoo enclosure.

We then cut to Hamish outside Miles's flat again – he has been tasked with finding out how Mrs Dawson is faring.

Hamish is welcomed in by Miles – Mrs Dawson is absent – and he and Miles sit at the kitchen table and talk about the union issues at work. They have a clash about ideology. Hamish thinks that the union should move with the times and staff should be more flexible about doing each other's jobs.

Miles slaps him down efficiently on all of this and takes an ideologically pure position every time.

They move off it and start talking about relationships instead.

'Do you ever get tempted?' says Hamish.

'By what? Money?'

'No. Women.'

'In my line of work you don't meet many,' Dawson says. 'It's a man's world. The odd secretary or typist. But they get gobbled up by the bosses.'

There is a knock on the door and Dawson asks Hamish to answer it, and when he swings the door open there is a huge surprise waiting for him.

It is the young man in the fawn leather jacket and cowboy boots – Miriam's other boyfriend.

This is the real 'oh oh' moment in the movie where the entire film audience at the time would have said out loud, *Oh my God, it's him. What's going to happen now?*

'Who are you?' the young man says, aggressively.

Hamish panics and doesn't know what to do, but then Miles comes out, sees the young man, and calls him in.

'Hi Ronnie,' he says and hugs him tight.

'Hamish, this is Ronnie.'

'Oh.'

'Ronnie is my son. He's been away for a while – if you know what I mean – but now he's back!'

Miles tells Ronnie how he met Hamish on the train when Hamish took him home after having a fit.

Ronnie Doors stares at Hamish in a cold way.

We can see that Hamish is horrified. Miles is having an affair with his son's girlfriend. And at this moment incriminating photographs of Miles and Miriam kissing and cavorting are being dropped into a postbox by Eva to end up on Mrs Dawson's lap. Hamish tries to make his excuses and leave but the father and son won't have any of it.

Cut to the three of them in a pub. Miles is at the bar and Ronnie is chatting to Hamish.

'I promote boxing. I've made a lot of money, lost a lot of money and made it all again. When you make a lot of money in a city like this, a city where everyone knows you, people think that they should have a bit of that money too. They think they are entitled to it. Don't look so shocked. It's boxing. It's not cricket on Bournville village green.'

Cut to a room backstage at a boxing club. In the background people are hitting punchbags. In the foreground men are putting coloured pills into little cellophane packets. It is smoky. A man is showing another man a gun and they are laughing.

Cut to ringside where the three of them are watching a match. The round ends and Ronnie chats to Hamish.

'Did you ever try to forget something that happened to you?' Ronnie says. 'Did you ever want to blank out a piece of your memory, silence it for ever? You can't. I've tried. It just can't be done. You hear a snatch of music, you smell something, or you see a particular turn in a road that looks like another turn in another road somewhere else, and you are back there right away. We didn't used to get on, you see, me and my dad. Partly why I changed my name. I went off the rails and had to spend some time living at Her Majesty's expense. You want to know what I did?'

'I'm not sure –'

'I killed a man. I have a temper and, I am sorry to say, I killed him. Over a business deal he cut me out of. Didn't mean to kill him, just starting hitting him and didn't stop. Luckily the judge decided it was involuntary manslaughter – else I'd still be rotting in there.'

'It's always business,' says Hamish. 'Or a woman.'

'If I found out anyone was messing around with my woman I worry that I would murder that man without a thought. I would be so furious, I would kill him with my own bare hands. I wouldn't pause to think. It wouldn't matter who it was. Even if it was my best friend, or my brother, if I had one. It wouldn't matter, the black fog would come down like last time, I just know it.'

Here we all feel we need to pause and have a think. We have a feeling we are being taken down to a dark and horrible place. And we are right. Film noir is a world where every man is a potential criminal, and monstrosity is something banal. It's not like in the old gangster films, where heinous acts are conveniently isolated in the criminal underworld; in film noir, evil is everywhere, lurking under the surface. And this is why 1940s film noir directors were fascinated with crime. Because it allowed them to investigate the nature of evil, and in particular, the way evil could in some way be ordinary, an ordinary part of ordinary people's ordinary lives. And it could be no coincidence, as I said in my essay for *Sight & Sound* magazine, that many of these film noir directors had fled from fascism and the Holocaust.

113

After the boxing club scene we cut to Hamish in a call box late at night.

'Is that you? Listen, whatever you do, don't send those pictures to Mrs Dawson.'

'What?'

Hamish listens, his face contorted into horror and amazement.

'Today?'

Close on his face contorting even further, his hand gripping the cord on the phone tighter and tighter, just as he does at the start of the film.

'Oh no. Peanut. Eva. You don't know what you've done. The young bloke we saw her with? You're right, he's the boxing promoter all right. *And he is some evil violent bastard who's already done time for killing a man. To make things worse, he is also Miles Dawson's son.*'

The camera follows Hamish's gaze through the window of the phone box and up to the dark sky. A plane passes by, its lights flashing. We see its wheels drop down. After it has passed, the camera stays on a slot of empty dark sky surrounded by clouds and we watch as the clouds slowly slide shut over this gap, and a forbidding change in the music announces a new, darker tone.

CHAPTER FOURTEEN

1988

The next morning I saw John Ireland in the paper shop with his wife and two kids and I was surprised to see he had a partner and family, as I had associated his multiple-garage-buying habit and his lone drinking with the life of a single man. When he was with his family he seemed much more cheery and he waved over at me and called out, 'Hi Daniel.'

'Hi,' I said. 'Are you enjoying the garage?'

'Very much so,' he said. 'Thanks a lot. You don't know how much it means to me.'

His wife was standing behind him. She was a tall thin woman with a pale, happy-looking face, and a dark black bob of hair. She was smiling and looked like one of those people who always smiled even when they were telling you something serious.

She rolled her eyes at me. 'I have no idea what goes on in his head,' she said. Then she put her hand on his shoulder. 'But if it makes him happy, what's the problem?'

Agnes was waiting outside my door.

'I can walk about now. I can go outside on my own. Look,' and she skipped over to the window, leaned her elbow on the ledge in a comedy nonchalant way, then hopped about the corridor like she was on a spring. Her face was almost clear of bruises and she was wearing the gauzy black floating blouse I had inhaled in her bedroom, along with crushed velvet trousers and white Chelsea boots. Her boots made me think about the pale-coloured wellingtons worn by the men who took Fiona away.

She was out of breath when she finally made me come back with her into her flat and we flopped down on her sofa, laughing. The real Agnes was emerging from behind her injuries.

'I wanted to tell you something,' she said. 'Everyone in the other block gets up early. Have you noticed that? And in this block, everyone gets up late.'

I didn't ask her how she knew what time everyone got up.

'It's like that block contains the opposite of this block. Have you ever thought about that?'

'Well,' I said. 'It's possible.'

Agnes looked shocked. 'Is it?'

'We are all controlled by invisible forces, aren't we?'

She moved away from me as if I had hit her.

'Are we?'

'Magnetism, gravity, electricity, radio waves, ultraviolet, infrared, heat, radiation. They say that people who live near pylons get depressed.'

Agnes rubbed her head and twisted her mouth into a comical, quizzical shape.

'Sometimes there's a rational explanation for weird stuff.'

She looked devastated. The thought that her ideas might be true, and worse, that they might have some basis in science rather than the occult.

'We get on, don't we,' she said, 'you and I?'

116

'Yes, I think we do.'

'It's like we know each other.'

Now that the bruising on her face had cleared up I could make out her features more easily and I found myself staring. Because there was something familiar about her that I couldn't place. Like when you see a person you know well, but because they are in a different context, you don't recognise them. Like seeing a teacher on the bus. She caught me staring and smiled. Then she took off her sunglasses for the first time and revealed her eyes. Greyish green with flecks of brown. They looked somehow younger than her body.

'You not worked it out yet, Quinn?'

'Did I go to school with you?'

'No. But you've seen me a lot. I have read everything you've written about me.' She put on a swaggery, slightly American accent. 'My name is Riain. Like Rain, but with an extra "i". Originally it was Ryan. Evaline Ryan. The Ni means born. I wanted to be a dancer for a while and I believed a new name would make me stand out.'

I didn't say anything.

'My first name is Agnes, but I never used that name professionally. Full name Agnes Mathilde Pelletier.' She stuck out her hand for shaking. 'Good to finally see you in person, Quinn, without that big screen between us.'

I was stunned. I sat there and stared at her face, taking it all in, and relating it to the contours of the images in the film I knew so well. A broken-off part of something had finally clicked into place.

'The papers said there was an accident on a motorbike.'

'We were racing and I turned out of the bend too soon. Met a truck who was as surprised as me. It's funny how hard you can be hit, and still get back up again.'

'Birmingham as a magnet for ex-film stars? Who knew?'

'When something good happens in a certain place, you go back there. Sometimes you keep going back. Like a lion cub going back to its dead mother for milk.'

'When does the cub give up?'

'It doesn't. Until another lioness turns up and takes it in.'

'John Ireland?'

'John's just a friend.'

Outside in the corridor I stood for a time, thinking. I looked from Agnes's front door to mine, and estimated the distance. A few yards, that was all. A few yards away from Eva Ni Riain, from Mathilde Pelletier. I paced the distance, counting the steps out loud. Eight yards, it was only eight yards.

The lift made a grumbling and whining sound as its steel wires dragged it up from the bottom of the block and the doors opened to reveal a policeman. He strode out quickly, and, seeing me standing there, immediately took a notebook out from his pocket.

'Sorry to disturb you,' he said, 'but we are investigating a missing child.'

PART TWO

PART TWO

CHAPTER ONE

1988

The policeman followed me into my flat and told me to sit down. He had a long nose and a face that was so thin I imagined it would become nothing more than a vertical line in the air if I looked at him straight on. But I never had a chance to see him like that because he jerked his head about all the time as if he were a bird searching in a cloud of invisible insects.

He explained that Betty had left the house at 10 a.m. after organising her mother's breakfast and sorting out the medication she needed for the day. Then her mother had heard the door go and the scooter wheels squeaking and hadn't heard from her since. When it got to four o'clock, the time when Betty usually wanted to watch the children's shows on the television, her mother got worried. She can't get to the phone herself so she banged on the floor to alert the neighbour below who came up and called the police. Betty had never done this sort of thing before. The policeman asked me when I had last seen her and what my relationship with her and her mother was. I was aware of his eyes roving about my flat, possibly wondering why it was so bare. And when I'd finished explaining my predicament and what had happened in Cumbria, and the way Betty had taken me over to Agnes's flat, and about Agnes falling down the stairs, he was silent for a time.

Then he said, 'Would you mind if I had a look around?'

Because I had been watching a lot of crime films I thought about saying, *Won't you need a warrant for that?* But then I thought of the scene in *Psycho* with the private detective Arbogast and Norman Bates, and wondered whether I was coming across twitchy and guilty-looking like Anthony Perkins in his classic performance.

'Of course, look around all you want,' I said, adding cheerily, 'you won't find anything untoward here,' making myself look even more shifty.

He took a few minutes to tour the flat, taking the longest time in the bathroom, and when he came back, he said, 'Why have you got that contraption made out of chairs on the balcony?'

'So I can see over,' I said.

'You like to watch people?'

'I suppose,' I said.

'When they are unaware of you watching?'

'No,' I said.

'But that's what you do.'

'Yes, I suppose that's what I do. But I don't like doing it.'

'So you are forced to do it? Something forces you to do it against your will?'

'No.'

'What is that something?'

I laughed. 'What something?'

'The something that forces you.'

'That something? I don't know, sir, I mean officer. I mean,

I just like to watch things while I am listening to records.'

He paused for a long time and looked at me.

'Were you watching today? At the time Betty disappeared?'

'I don't know. Because I don't know what time she disappeared. I was watching a film before I went over to see Agnes.'

'She your new girlfriend?'

'She's older than me,' I said.

'Doesn't mean she can't be your girlfriend.'

'Well, I know, but she isn't.'

'Then just say that she isn't. It will make life easier for us both if you answer the questions simply, Mr Quinn, and not add other facts which confuse everything.' He took a breath. 'OK. So, normally Betty takes you over to Agnes's flat, but today you went on your own?'

'Yes.'

'And you haven't seen Betty at all?'

'No.'

I didn't tell him about the day I saw her getting on a bus to Worcester. Because this would have involved explaining why I had been sitting on the number 11 bus for three hours on my own.

'Whose is the lipstick in the bathroom?'

'Children don't wear lipstick.'

'Woah, woah there. Slow down. You're at it again.'

'Oh sorry. Yes. That belongs to Agnes.'

'Does she know she left it here?'

'I'll take it round to her later.'

'Want me to take it over to her? I'm going to question her next.'

'No. It's OK.'

He stared at me for a few moments.

'OK,' he said, finally.

The policeman was still talking with Mathilde an hour later when more policemen and policewomen arrived and asked everyone from the block to gather outside to help in the search for Betty. I thought it was odd that the police didn't include the other block in the community effort and thought about what Mathilde had said about that block being the opposite of this one. Maybe if this block is the one that loses people, that block might be the one that finds them. But I don't think that idea would have made sense to the police so I didn't mention it.

We were given electric torches and rough instructions on how to divide up so that we covered every area. We looked in every stairwell, down every passage, up every alley, in every clump of bushes and every empty building, but nothing was found. Not even her scooter. The local TV news put out an item along with a picture of her and called for any sightings to be reported, and sightings came in, but all of them were untrue, or even deliberate hoaxes. I was distraught. I felt I knew little Betty so well. I knew how clever she was and how capable. She was trusting – too trusting possibly. With her cheery catchphrases, 'see you later, navigator' and 'compliance'. She would be happy to chat away to strangers and tell them everything about herself and her mother, but innocently unaware of any of the risks this sharing of information could bring. She would help anyone who told her they were in trouble, like the way she helped Agnes – or Mathilde rather – taking long phone messages for her and running to and fro. How easily she might be coerced by someone to go somewhere she didn't want to go or do something she didn't want to do.

*

I bought a kebab from the Ghost Chilli takeaway on the other side of the Yew Tree and ate it in the cold on my balcony. A lorry with a large load was moving slowly up the slip road to the M6. It was straddling two lanes and a long queue of traffic had formed behind it. The load looked like the wooden structure for a roof or part of a boat. I looked down and saw John Ireland walk up the street and over to his now wholly owned row of black garages. He opened up his new acquisition with the key I had given him and I was glad to see that it worked because I hadn't even opened it myself to see what was in there. It was an up-and-over door and he reached in and flipped a switch and light flooded the space. But I couldn't see from that distance what was in there. He didn't go inside, just looked into it for a long time and then closed the door again, locked the padlock, and after a long pause, patted the door of the garage as if it were the flank of a much-loved animal. There was a noticeable spring in his step when he set off down the road to his flat in the other block.

A chain was unhooked, then another, then a bolt slid back, then another, then I heard the clunk of a big key opening a deadlock, then another, and finally the door opened a crack and Mathilde's face looked out at me.

'It's been over twenty-four hours now,' I said.

'Come in.'

She poured me a whisky and sat me down.

'I thought you'd want to probe me a bit more about the film.'

'I can't think about it.'

'Betty will be safe. I know it in my bones. She is a strong and sensible girl.'

'Has anyone looked over there?' I nodded towards the window.

'Where?'

'The garages.'

Mathilde took in a long breath and shook her head. 'A man acts a little differently to other men and everyone think the worst.'

'She could have got trapped. She could have got inside one of the garages and it could have locked behind her.'

'The police asked John to check them and he did, and he told the police that there were no signs that she had been there.'

Mathilde stood up quickly and lifted the large screwdriver off the floor. 'Come on.'

I was in shirtsleeves and it was freezing cold outside. We tried the handles of the garages and knocked hard on the doors, but nothing came back.

'Which one is yours?' said Mathilde.

I indicated the one on the far end and she went over, inserted her screwdriver between the door and the wall, and began to prise it open. The lock looked like it was about to snap when we heard a voice and turned to see John Ireland walking briskly towards us.

He was out of breath when he reached us. 'Agnes. Your health is much improved,' he said.

She threw the screwdriver on to the floor with a clatter and walked away, leaving me and John Ireland together.

'The weird man who wants all the garages must be collecting small girls and tying them up in there,' said John. 'Come on then.' He slid the key into my garage lock and threw the up-and-over door open violently, making a loud clanking sound. Inside it was dark. A foul smell of oil and damp seeped out. He switched on the light to reveal that it was completely empty, and then he opened up the next one and it was empty too and when he went to open the third I stopped him.

'It's fine. It's just we are all so worried. I'm sure you are too. You have children. She was such a lovely little girl.'

'*Is*,' said John. '*Is* a lovely little girl.'

CHAPTER TWO

1988

Later that evening I was asleep on the sofa when the letter-box rattled. I sat up and listened intently, as I believed I was half dreaming. But it went again. No one else had tried to attract my attention in that way. I thought of ghosts or other strange phenomena and went over to the door and waited near it. The letterbox rattled again, and the rhythm and the way it went was exactly the same as when Betty had done it.

I turned the knob slowly and pulled the door open a crack. It was a woman with long grey hair, a nose piercing, and black motorcycle boots. I opened the door further and saw that at her side was little Betty, holding the woman's hand, and grinning. She was wearing the same heavy jeans with the large turn-ups, the same thick jumper, and she was carrying her scooter.

'Betty said she wanted to come and say hello, and tell you she was safe.'

'Oh my God,' I said, 'they found you!' I thought of hugging her but it didn't seem right when she wasn't my child and I was a lone man who could possibly be perceived as a threat to her.

'I'm Gill from Sandwell Social Services,' the woman said. 'This sometimes happens with young carers. Tell Mr Quinn where you went, Betty.'

'I went to the zoo. Dudley Zoo. I wanted to see the giraffe. He's called Donald. I saw him on the news and they said he was dying. I thought I might be able to help him because he has things wrong with him like my mum has.'

'She went there – didn't you, Betty – on her own – three buses – and spent all day looking at the animals and then she got locked in. Slept in the café and was found by a cleaner the next day.'

'Poor Donald is dying,' Betty said. 'I thought I'd be able to help, but they said he was getting the right medicine and they were doing everything they could. But he was lying down and giraffes are not supposed to be lying down, even I know that. After I saw Donald I saw the chimps and the monkeys and the polar bear and the snakes and even eagles and owls. It's not fair the way some of the animals are kept there. They don't look happy, some of them, and the buildings they are in are all concrete and cold-looking. Like living round here. It was good though, Mr Quinn, I enjoyed it, but I've learned my lesson so I won't go off on my own again. *Compliance.*'

'Mr Quinn,' Gill the social worker went on, 'we have explained to Betty and her mother about respite care and about how we can arrange for Betty to have a few days out at weekends with kids of her own age. It's all possible and will do her good. Let's just thank God that she's safe and sound.'

The next morning I stopped outside my block and stared at the other block of flats. The two blocks never looked right when you saw them together; they were like uneasy identical twins who had been introduced in later life and had never got used to the fact that the other one existed. What if that block of flats was indeed, as Mathilde had speculated, an inversion of the one I lived in? Maybe there was a version of me in there as well, always doing the opposite of what I was doing. Maybe in that block, in that flat, in number 69, maybe in there, everything was the same as it had been before everything changed. Maybe in that block, my flat was still empty, and I was still in Cumbria with Fiona.

I decided to go to the bus station at Digbeth. I wanted to watch the National Express to west Cumbria leave the station at 13.26, as it did every day. That was the one we had taken together that day a few months ago.

CHAPTER THREE

1987

It was the end of the summer holidays and we had graduated from our respective courses and were between homes because our tenancy on the house in Chuckery had run out. So we had decided to spend the summer in Cumbria with my parents. We would sign on as unemployed and claim benefits and while we were there we would decide where we wanted to go next. What we wanted to do together. It would be a welcome break from the busy city and also Fiona wanted to spend some time walking in the mountains, which I had promised I would do with her, even though I didn't really have any interest in scenery.

On the coach Fiona asked me hundreds of questions about my family in west Cumbria. Was my mother a farmer's wife type who baked cakes all day and had animals running around her feet while she skipped about in a pinny with her hair in a scarf and her cheeks forever pink from the fresh air, and always offering everyone tea and titbits from a massive Aga oven?

'No, she isn't like that,' I said. 'It's not like that where I live.'

'Are there sheep and fields?'

'Well, yes,' I said. 'But there's also a nuclear plant and a chemical factory and council estates.'

The National Express coach took a long time, but as neither of us had a job, it seemed the best and cheapest way to get up there. It took seven and a half hours and stopped several times on the way to its final destination, Whitehaven, where it would deposit us, and where we had to get a local bus to Cleator Moor where my parents were.

My mother had unwrapped a Battenburg cake and my father had put on a jacket and tie and we sat down in the front room which was for reserved for guests and entertaining. We drank our tea while they asked Fiona lots of questions. My mother and father hadn't travelled much and had never been to Birmingham so they asked her lots of questions about what it was like living in a big, noisy city. They asked her about the IRA bomb; where was she when it went off? When she told them she was at the Odeon watching *Planet of the Apes*, right next to the site of the bombing, the Mulberry Bush pub, at the bottom of the Rotunda, their mouths fell open in shock and amazement.

And when she told them she had been up to Cumbria many times with her family to go walking up the fells they were very impressed. My mother and father never went up the fells. They thought the fells were bleak and depressing. They liked lakes though – but strangely they didn't like the sea. They thought the sea was bleak and depressing as well. Which was odd, they laughed, because lakes and the sea are kind of the same thing apart from the size. But nevertheless, lakes were definitely more their thing. As children, they told Fiona, a highlight of the year was a school trip to the shore of Ennerdale Water.

I sat quietly, watching her interact with them. I am an only child – the sole recipient of my parents' love – so this additional person was like extending the family in a real sense. It was great to see them take so much interest in her and leave me alone for a while, to be honest. Usually my visits home consisted of endless questions about what I was doing with my life. When was I going to begin some sort of career? Preferably as a teacher. My mother (because she was a teacher, and all her friends, and a lot of her family members, were teachers) always felt that everyone should be a teacher and if they deviated from that norm they were required to explain why. *Did you ever think about teaching?* she would always say, after someone had explained in detail what job they did.

That night we borrowed my dad's car and went to St Bees where we walked along the beach and laughed about my mother's questions and how she thought that maybe Fiona could be a music teacher, what with all her qualifications. The last thing Fiona wanted was to be in a room full of squealing children. It would be like being in a horrible sound installation by Simon Slatcher, a tattooed hulk of a boy who studied composition with her and created what he called 'sonic assaults'.

It was dusk, and the tide was turning, the sea shrinking away from the pebble beach and crawling back over the sand towards the horizon, exposing a fringe of weed and debris. We stood holding hands and looked out into the darkening clouds and the white frothing waves. We listened to the sound of pebbles being dragged to and fro as the waves pushed and pulled them in and out. I felt as though we were blessed. The first couple to ever feel in love and look out over an empty beach on a dusky evening with no one else about. We listened to the wind, and we listened to the waves, and we decided that these sounds were important. In our noses we got the prickly, bitter smell of the sea, infused with coal smoke from the village behind us. We began to feel cold as the damp rose up around us from the soggy ground.

We went to a pub at St Bees and shared a pie and chips and drank beer. Afterwards we parked my father's car down a dirt track and sat in the pitch dark for a time. We talked about how everyone's parents were always eccentric and weird, and about how we would also be weird when we were old and how our children, if we ever had any, would laugh at us and do impressions of us for their friends. We would have catchphrases. Like *is this radiator on?* That would be mine. Or, for Fiona, *have you ever thought about getting a slow cooker?* We climbed into the back of the car and kissed for a while. Fiona managed to hitch up her skirt and pull down her tights. She undid my jeans, took out my cock and helped me enter her. She sat astride me and rocked slowly to and fro and I looked up at where her face would be but it was so dark all I could see was the heavy-looking black sky filled with tiny white stars and I felt her moving to and fro and she did this for a few minutes and all I did was look at the stars while she moved on me. Then she shuddered and came, giving out a loud animal growl as she did so which I was sure the sheep in the field behind us would have been able to hear. I felt myself about to come and used my hands on her hips to indicate she should move off and she did. We used no contraception at that point – she had given up on the pill because it made her feel funny, and neither of us liked the smell of condoms. She stroked me with her fingers till it was ended and we lay in the back of the car and looked at the stars and I felt that I was the happiest I had ever been and wondered if we could be frozen together in this state for

134

ever because I never really ever wanted to be anywhere else or be with anyone else or be doing anything else than there, with her, then.

The next day there was a do for my mother's retirement from her job as deputy head of the local primary school, St Patrick's, and we had to attend, of course. The kids had made a banner and the teachers had hung it outside. It had coloured crepe paper stuck all over it in rosette shapes and said *Goodbye Mrs Quinn, we'll miss you* in glittery letters.

The hall was full of parents. On the stage dozens of small children were standing ready to sing, their arms tightly by their sides, feet neatly together, their little heads tilted sideways towards my mother who was sitting at the piano readying herself to play. It seemed odd that she would provide the music for her own send-off. My mother nodded at the choir and played the first note and the children opened their mouths wide to sing.

Goodbye Old Paint
I'm a-leaving Cheyenne

The children's little voices strained for the notes, and they were discordant and out of tune with each other, and the words of the song seemed strange and mournful and I didn't really understand them. A horse called Old Paint was leaving its owner. Or dying. Or was the owner leaving it to perish in a home for old horses?

Old Paint's a good pony and she paces when she can
We lay down on the blankets of the green grassy ground
And the horses and the cattle were grazing all around
In the middle of the ocean there grows a green tree
But it falls to the girl that loves me

The strange muddled sentiments of the song collided inside me, causing a flood of unaccountable despair and grief, and I had to pinch the top of my nose to stem the tears. Looking back, it was as if the emotion had somehow hit me before the event, like the way the light from a star can reach the earth millions of years after it has died.

I rushed outside and stood in the cold, looking up at the dark cloudless sky.

There were speeches. I could hear the PA whistling and the applause, but none of the content. Then I heard massive cheers and whoops and I guessed it was the end and so I crept back in, my temporary departure unnoticed. My mother was on the stage, crying, a big bunch of flowers in her hand. She gathered herself together and went up to the microphone and said a few words, but she was too upset to give a whole speech, even though I knew she had written one. She'd been teaching at the school her whole life – her one and only job – so it meant a lot to her.

Outside we gathered for photographs and then it was back to our house for cups of tea, salmon vol-au-vents, and tinned mandarin oranges with Carnation milk.

I watched the 13.26 coach to Cumbria roll out of its bay, the rumble of diesel and the hiss of its brakes filling the coach station with noise as it paused before pulling into the traffic, and I thought of the words again.

In the middle of the ocean there grows a green tree
But it falls to the girl that loves me
This time I knew why I was crying.

CHAPTER FOUR

1988

Watching the next section of *Out of the Dark* I felt a very peculiar sensation every time Mathilde Pelletier came on the screen. I now knew her. I had spoken to her. She was my neighbour. She lived eight yards away from me.

This was the part just after the scene in which Hamish realises that Eva has sent the photographs to Miles's wife. Hamish and Eva know that there is no way back. And that is one of the key factors of a good film noir. It is the doing of things that cannot be undone. That is the engine of these films, that is what propels the characters to make more and more dangerous and irreversible decisions, decisions that take them further and further out into the unknown, and deeper and deeper into morally ambiguous and psychologically warped reality, a world of horror and lust, of murder, and lies, of guilt and despair. And we know that's where Hamish and Eva are heading – we just don't know the route they will take to get there. And that's why we watch – because we want to find out.

In the next section, Hamish and Eva lie low for a while to see what happens. They agree no contact with each other.

At this point in the film, if you are in a cinema, you can almost hear the audience's attention deepen.

There is a wordless montage sequence of cross-cuts between the two characters, with the deep and complex music of Penderecki drenched all over it.

Eva alone in a high-class expensive boutique, trying on clothes.

Hamish prowling about his house, smoking, looking for something on a long shelf of books about unions and management and industrial politics.

Eva wriggling into a narrow black cocktail dress before slipping her feet into a pair of three-inch heels.

Hamish with his children, playing in a park on some swings.

A long overhead shot of Eva walking down the street and going into a bar; the same bar that Hamish was in with Ronnie and Miles.

Hamish in his office at the plant.

Shop floor – cars being assembled.

Hamish in a union meeting where the union reps and management are shouting at each other. The room is full of cigarette smoke and cans of beer.

Eva shaving her legs in a luxurious bath while summery pop music plays.

Hamish buying newspapers then walking by a canal, Gas Street Basin, anxiously scouring the headlines before throwing every copy into the water.

Eva in a cocktail bar, her cigarette in a long holder, laughing loudly with someone we don't see.

Hamish with his wife, eating a meal in silence. Grey blocks of meat, dry mashed potato, shrivelled peas. A clock ticking. Knives and forks clinking on plates.

Cut to the window. It starts to rain. And when it rains in film noir, that's when you know trouble is coming.

It's the middle of the night and Hamish gets an anguished call from Eva. He pretends to his wife it's a union issue.

Hamish gets to Eva's place and he finds Eva crying hysterically.

She points to the kitchen.

He runs in and finds Miles's son, Ronnie, lying on the floor bleeding. He is alive but dying. He can hardly speak.

'We have to get him to a hospital,' says Hamish.

'No. He came here to kill you, Hamish. He found out about me and you spying on him. Somehow he found my address. He wouldn't listen. We tussled in the kitchen and I grabbed a kitchen knife – to defend myself – and he stumbled on to it. If we save him, he'll kill you. Kill you for telling his mother about his girlfriend and Miles. For messing about with his life. Then he'll kill Miriam. Then, of course, he'll kill Miles.'

The dying man tries to say something and the camera goes in close to his face. Blood is trickling down the sides of his chin.

'Help me, help me.'

'Don't listen to him,' says Eva.

'It's her, she's evil,' Ronnie says in a husky, barely understandable voice.

'He is talking about Miriam,' Eva says. 'Finish him, Hamish. If you're big enough. If you are man enough. If you love me. Finish him for me.'

Hamish grabs a cushion and holds it over Ronnie's face.

Ronnie's legs kick for a few long seconds, and the sound of his shoes clopping on the wooden floor and sight of them twitching is horrific. The shot seems very prolonged. Then the kicking stops. In the struggle Hamish has got himself covered in the man's blood.

What was Hamish thinking here, you might ask. Well that's a question that doesn't seem to work with these sorts of films. Film noir undermines a key principle of classical drama – the notion that people are in control of their actions. Instead, characters in film noir are propelled by mysterious, buried forces that even they themselves don't seem to understand.

Hamish tells Eva to go. Get out of town for a while.

She grabs a coat and goes into the bedroom where a suitcase is already packed, its lid standing up showing clothes neatly arranged inside it.

Cut to Hamish standing and staring at Ronnie's dead body.

Cut to Eva sitting on the bed looking at her watch, her hand on the handle of the now closed suitcase.

Cut to Hamish looking out of the window, at some drunks walking along, laughing and singing.

Eva comes out of the bedroom with her suitcase and gives Hamish a long sensual kiss.

We see a close-up of her hand slipping into Hamish's pocket and she takes out a card, a business card. She crumples it in her hand and her kisses become more passionate. Then we see her slip the business card into Ronnie's jacket pocket before she leaves.

Finally, we see her screeching away in a sporty car we haven't seen before.

Hamish spots a black leather wallet on the mantlepiece, opens it, and puts it into his own pocket. Then he wraps the body up in a rug and drags it into the hall. He looks out through the glass in the front door, checking the coast is clear, then he opens the door and drags the rug outside.

He has it by the boot of his car when a couple come around the corner, drunk and staggering about. They stop at the rug on the pavement.

'You doing a moonlight flit, mate?'

'Just getting rid of some old stuff we don't need,' Hamish says. 'Those old Victorian rugs our parents had. Depressing.'

'Want a hand?' the man says, then bends to pick up the carpet, but can't.

'Bloody hell, mate. That's one heavy piece of floor covering.'

'It's OK, I'll manage,' says Hamish. 'You get yourselves back where it's warm inside.'

Cut to Hamish at the Longbridge plant. He uses a key to enter a goods yard where he finds a large heavy plastic sack, some rope, and some heavy engine parts. He drags all these to his car and puts them into the boot with Ronnie's body.

He locks the gates of the Longbridge plant behind him, all the while scouring the street to make sure no one has seen him.

Shots of slapping windscreen wipers and pattering rain, Hamish's pale serious face reflected in the windscreen, mixed with blurred city lights, and rivulets of rainwater.

He drives for miles out of Birmingham and up to a reservoir. Gasometers in the background. In the boot he has a dinghy, a kids' dinghy you use on the beach, and he gets it out and pumps it up. This seems to take ages. He puts Ronnie's corpse into a plastic sack with the engine parts for weight and ties it with the ropes. Then Hamish and the body float out on the black water in the black moonless night.

He has a small electric torch in his teeth and the light from this dances about on the water like a firefly. At one point he drops the torch and has to scramble madly for it to stop it going into the water.

He sends Ronnie's body over the side into the water at a point in the middle, where he thinks the reservoir is deepest.

He takes the torch from between his teeth and sits back in the dinghy for a few moments and watches the water.

The camera pushes past Hamish and focuses on the ripples on the surface where the sack has just gone in and we see a couple of bubbles rise up and we keep watching this black surface wondering whether the body will bob up again out of it. But nothing happens. The image becomes stiller and stiller until the water is merely a sheet of blackness slowly flexing in the night.

Dreams about reservoirs and darkness and floating dead bodies disturbed my sleep so from early the next morning I had been sitting on my balcony looking out at the motorway junction and listening to records. It must have been around midday (I remember the *Straw Dogs* soundtrack was playing at the time) when something, a movement, or a sound possibly, drew my eye from the motorway to John Ireland's garages, and I was surprised to see Betty's zebra-striped scooter leaning against the black door at the end of the row. The garage that used to be mine, in fact. I watched for a few minutes and eventually Betty appeared from behind the garages. She had a rucksack in her hand and dangling from it was an orange vacuum flask. I thought about calling down to her but decided not to. I didn't want to draw attention to myself. I felt in a privileged position high up here looking down on everything – like a sniper who could see every target – and for some reason, I didn't want to give away my position, even to this small child.

Betty flipped the rucksack on to her shoulder, planted her foot on the scooter and glided off down the road past the empty green area and out of sight. I wondered whether I should run down and follow her, make sure she was safe, but following a twelve-year-old girl might make me seem a bit odd, so I dropped that idea. She was probably just off to the shops on an errand. But what was she doing round the back of the garages? I made a mental note to make sure I knocked on her mother's door later to check she had returned safely. Then I remembered her mother wasn't able to come to the door. Also she had no phone and at this point my train of thought ran into the buffers and to be honest I forgot all about her and my mind wandered back on to my own concerns. Later I was meeting Mathilde and for the first time we were to have a proper chat, tête-à-tête.

CHAPTER FIVE

1988

A shopping arcade called Oasis World had been built on
the site of the Hollow Egg, full of traders in vintage clothes,
old furniture, second-hand records, musty overcoats, garish
band T-shirts, leather belts and bags. Echo and the Bunny-
men and the Cure played there all day. The café was called
the Centenary Lounge, and in one half of it there were
four-seat vinyl booths, and in the other half a long Formica
counter with a row of swivel stools. At the far end of this
counter sat Eva Ni Riain.

But this wasn't Eva Ni Riain. This was Mathilde Pelletier; a struggling French actor who had never found her
feet after the sixties. And my nearest neighbour. As I ap-
proached, she stood up and stared at me hard, as if she was
seeing me for the first time, tilting her head on one side and
raising her eyebrows at the same time. I realised I had never seen her outside the flats before and was surprised she
existed in this plane of reality, as if she were a creature of
a very specialised habitat, like a fish that lives only in mud.
With her injuries almost healed, she was like a completely
different person.

'You know what? You're not bad-looking. When I first read one of your articles I pictured someone more studi-ous-looking. All that highfalutin stuff you write about that old film. Existentialist-this and nihilistic-that.'

She placed her chin into her gloved hand and pushed her face close to me.

'The female gaze,' she crooned at me, swivelling her face this way and that and making her eyes pop open wide. 'Freud and his suppressed sexuality. I can tell you, Quinn – when we were making that film no one suppressed anything. Sit down here next to me.'

I did as she asked.

'Betty went to Dudley Zoo,' I said.

'I know.'

'Coincidence?'

'Why?'

'It's in the film.'

'Must be one of Julian's scenes. I only know my own scenes.'

'Oh yes. They used to say you only ever read your own part of the script.'

'Isn't that true of us all?'

'Maybe you should watch it with me.'

'Maybe I should pull my eyes out and eat them with pickles.'

A plump waitress with ginger hair came over and asked for our order.

'A bottle of Fino, please,' Mathilde said.

'What's Fino?' the waitress and I said in unison.

'White sherry. Bone-dry fortified wine. That's the drink for us today.'

'Isn't sherry for old aunties at Christmas?'

'Pfaw! I lived in Spain for a time, trust me. Do you have it, miss?'

The waitress blushed until her skin matched her hair.

'I'll have a look,' she said and dashed off.

Now that Mathilde was out of the flat and no longer the helpless invalid she had been when I met her a few weeks ago, I could really look at her properly. She appeared to have dressed up for the occasion and everything she was wearing was black and extreme. A long coat with a fur collar, a tight-fitting dress made of crushed velvet, a necklace of feathers and pearls, and a small hat that I think you would call a pillbox with a small piece of net at the front. I wondered if she could lower this dramatic curtain the way a Sicilian widow might at a gangster's funeral. On her legs she had long high-heeled boots which fitted her calves tightly and were shiny like they were made of plastic. She looked as though she had become trapped inside the character of Eva Ni Riain and was unable to escape.

The waitress brought over a green bottle with waves of frosty mist curling off it, opened it, and placed the cork next to it on the table. Two small tumblers were found, the drinks were poured, and we chinked glasses and sipped.

Mathilde looked at me for a long time, then made her voice go husky, low-pitched and as crackly as an old soundtrack.

'It's a game, Hamish, only a game,' she said.

I laughed and took another swig of sherry, feeling it sharp and cold and sour in my throat.

'Can I win?' I said.

'Of course not. Play a game with me and you can only lose. But you can lose well or you can lose badly.'

'And if I lose badly?'

146

'You lose everything.'

'And if I lose well?'

'You lose only yourself. But maybe losing yourself is what you really want. Ha ha ha – you've got it word for word, Quinn.'

We laughed again, chinked glasses, and refilled them.

She leaned back in her seat, stretching out her long boots. 'When we made that picture, the film that you claim is so deep and complex, we were just making a yarn, a piece of entertaining fluff. That's all it was. If you'd been on the set you'd have known there was no art there. Otto shouting and swearing at everyone, me and Julian forgetting our lines, everyone turning up on set high, or drunk, or just hungover – it's a surprise we got anything in the can at all.' She played with her hair and looked into the middle distance. The waitress brought us biscuits to go with our drinks and Mathilde dipped hers in the sherry and nibbled at it while smiling at me.

The hours went and so did the sherry – two bottles I think – and Mathilde Pelletier didn't stop talking for a single second. She talked about the movie business and the various low-rent flicks she'd made since *Out of the Dark*. She talked about the dodgy drug dealers and criminals she'd known in the sixties. She talked about the men and husbands she'd found, loved and lost, and about the superficiality of the entertainment world and how it was corrupt and a sham and out to destroy you. She told me about all the locations from the film, how certain shots had been made and what had been cut out, and when I pushed her further, she went through every name she could remember – real names, character names, and names of the crew. But none of them sounded right.

147

When she took a breath I changed the subject.

'Did you really fall down those stairs?'

Mathilde tapped a cigarette out from a pack of Gitanes and her brow furrowed as she lit it.

'Or maybe you arrived in that state one rainy night. In a taxi or something. Like the start of a film.'

She blew a stream of smoke up towards the ceiling and looked at me as if she was going back a long way. 'You, Quinn, would love my other place in Birmingham. Big art deco block like an ocean liner.'

'Stairs just as hard, though?'

She shook her head and smiled, then stood up. 'I want us to leave separately if that's OK.'

The half-smoked cigarette got crushed into her empty sherry glass, then she picked biscuit crumbs from her lips with gloved fingers while looking at herself in a small brass compact. 'You are right. There is more to my plight than what is on the surface.' She snapped the compact shut and slid it into her coat pocket. 'But nothing for you to worry about. I just need to be careful.'

After she had left the café I sat there on my own. I called the ginger waitress over and ordered some toast and a cup of tea.

I liked it in there. I liked the shy ginger waitress. I imagined that she would never ask you anything about what you were doing that day, or who you were, what you did for a job, or where you lived. It was a place where people without pasts or people without futures could drift in and out and would neither be remembered nor expected. Or missed if they never returned. But during the short spell you were there, you felt as if you'd been noticed and that you meant something at the time.

My tea came and the waitress plonked it down.

'There you are!'

The radio played 'Ghost Town'.

In a booth opposite, a man in a black polo-neck was drinking an espresso from a tiny cup.

In the next booth an older couple were sharing a toasted teacake.

A cleaner was pushing debris around the floor with a brush.

I thought back to Cumbria, after it had happened. I was in a small waiting area outside the ward, and I had my hand over my face in what seems now an overdramatic pose. But that's what I did. I sat with my hand like this for a while as if I didn't feel I ought to remove it until someone had come and asked me if I was OK. What sort of world was it that someone could sit with their hand over their face, clearly in great distress, and no one would come and ask them how they were doing? I began to think about how time was passing while I sat like this and realised it was very difficult to measure time when you had no reference points. I heard things while I was sitting like this – feet scraping on the floor, the door squeaking as it opened and shut, bleeps and hisses from the machinery in the ward. A cleaner came near me with her mop and bucket and I saw her feet through my fingers but I still didn't move.

Eventually a nurse tapped me on the shoulder.

'Mr Quinn, Mr Quinn?'

I took my hand away and looked up at her.

'I know it's difficult,' she said. 'Do you need anything? Can we help? Do you need a taxi home? It's three in the morning.'

'I need to go away for a few days,' I said. 'And I'm worried about it. If I go away for a few days, will she be OK?'

149

'She's doing fine. She'll probably be in here for another few months. She needs that time to get to full strength. If you need to be away, that's fine. Just ring us every day and we'll give you an update. There's really nothing you can do here at the moment. We are giving her the best care here she could ever get. She's in the best place. Just go, Mr Quinn.'

'Yes. I really need to go.'

'Here's our card with a number on it. We answer that number twenty-four hours a day. Ring any time you are worried, any time at all. We don't mind. And of course if anything changes we will call you on whatever number you give us.'

I rummaged in my pocket and found a number for Fiona's mum and dad who were storing my things.

I stared at my tea. It had gone cold. Butter had dripped off my toast and congealed into hard patches of yellow on my plate.

CHAPTER SIX

1988

It was cold on the balcony, too cold to watch the motorway any longer, which had become very quiet anyway, so I went inside and switched on the video player.

I had left the film at the scene where Hamish was at home washing off the blood. After this there is an abrupt cut to Hamish in his garden the next day burning his clothes on a bonfire, followed by the famous close-up of his shoe with blood stains on the heel. Then cut to Hamish walking by the canal. He takes out the black wallet that we saw him remove from Eva's flat and we see him take out the contents one by one and send them fluttering into the canal. A banknote, a scrap of paper with a number on it, a business card, a handwritten receipt. Then a photograph, which Hamish stares at for a time, and the camera pushes into it so that it momentarily fills the screen. A small boy with his father. They are on a merry-go-round, sitting in a tin spaceship, and the father is grinning at the camera while the boy is looking up at him, and laughing. Hamish flips this photograph into the canal and we then see it in close-up as it floats on the water for a few moments, then the water washes over it and it disappears just as Ronnie's body had disappeared into the reservoir.

Then a series of cutaways showing Hamish and Eva doing different things.

Hamish and Florence are at Dudley Zoo with the kids. Everything he sees at the zoo reminds him of what he has done. Murder, death, violence. He sees dead meat being fed to a lion. He sees a snake digesting something large in its stomach. He watches a chimpanzee banging its chest in anger. He is shown staring at the enclosures, but when we flip to his point of view, the focus is pulled back to the bars, the walls, the netting, the cages themselves. There are close-ups of zookeepers' hands locking and unlocking the pens. The horrendous clangs of slamming cage doors fill the soundtrack. A polar bear paces up and down, psychotically. There is a close-up of a giraffe's neck, bloody and cut where it has been repeatedly rubbing against the walls of its enclosure. The wails of monkeys and the whooping of wolves sound like sirens. Finally, a close-up of a baboon's garish face fills the screen and then cuts abruptly to a matching shot of a human face covered in what looks like dark mud. Pull back to reveal Eva in a face mask. She is in a beauty salon, wearing a fluffy white towel, smoking and laughing with the beauticians.

Back to Hamish home from the zoo, sitting on his own in the kitchen, trying to concentrate on a book on industrial relations, while his wife Florence is drinking something from a tumbler and swaying awkwardly to 'Johnny Remember Me', playing on a Dansette. She moves over to Hamish and tries to distract him, and get him to dance with her. He pushes her away and she stomps out of the room drunkenly and goes upstairs on her own.

Cut to Eva looking glamorous, smoking in front of a mirror.

Now that I had met the actress in person, each time I saw her character on the screen I felt a strange closeness to her. A stronger sense of her dangerousness. And at the same time a new sense of her vulnerability. You see, I didn't feel as though I had met Mathilde Pelletier at all. I felt as though I had met Eva Ni Riain. And I now felt as if the film were infecting my real life, as if I was entering the film, or the film was entering me. Was I becoming Hamish and being pulled into the same whirlpool of deceit and corruption and death and despair, with Eva Ni Riain at its centre?

Cut to Hamish walking the streets. He stops and looks through a window at a children's party. The camera noses into a close-up of the birthday kid's happy face and the other kids all singing and clapping. Everything seems so far away from the place Hamish is in, like he is watching from underwater, and this effect is enhanced by the tone washes and the music on the soundtrack, a dissonant drone that throbs beneath the kids singing 'Happy Birthday', drowning out the words.

Happy birthday dear Daniel, I thought, thinking about what Mathilde had said.

Cut to Hamish and Florence far apart lying in bed looking at the ceiling.

Eva on the phone to someone, her face serious.

Then a shot of the reservoir at night and a group of police divers. Torch beams searching in the murky depths.

A wobbly circle of light picks out the plastic sack which has landed on a ledge.

The diver swims over and opens the top of the bag.

Ronnie Doors's face looks back at them.

Cut to them searching the body at the station. A policeman puts a hand into Ronnie Doors's jacket and pulls out the card we saw Eva put in there.

Hamish McGrath,

Assistant Chief Accountant,

Longbridge Motor Plant

A montage follows, with no dialogue or sound effects, just Penderecki's ponderous, atonal music.

A spinning newspaper stops −

BOXING PROMOTER MURDERED

− and we squirm at the focus on the profession of the victim. A taxi driver poisoned, a teacher shot, a literary agent stabbed, an antique dealer clubbed, a prostitute strangled. Never a mother, a brother, an Elvis fan, or a collector of porcelain owls. Newspaper readers know that boxing is corrupt and will assume he's been murdered by a rival promoter or a boxer paid to take a dive.

But this time the boxing business has nothing to do with it.

Cut to Hamish being interviewed. He puts his head in his hands.

A policeman closes a large notebook with a snap and leaves him alone.

Hamish in the court.

In the public gallery Miles Dawson and Mrs Dawson, both wearing black, weeping.

Florence, Hamish's wife, is staring straight ahead, looking dazed.

Eva is in the witness stand, dressed in black. She points at Hamish and then puts her head in her hands and weeps. She is taken away from the stand.

The jury returns and gives the verdict.

We see Hamish hang his head in desperation. Then he is

taken away, violently protesting and shouting his innocence to the world.

At this point the audience is appalled. If you are lucky enough to catch it in a cinema you can almost hear the sighs of outrage. A man who is basically good and well-meaning will go to prison. But this is film noir. This is the moral world of film noir. Stray from the path, just once, only once, and you can easily lose everything, for ever, with no chance of redemption. Poor Hamish is pulled into the whirlpool of Eva's charms and he drowns himself there. Lured by the prospect of sinful pleasure, he ends up suffering terrifying retribution. And there's no reprieve in film noir. In a film noir you pay and pay and pay – for sins you were made to commit by someone else.

What follows is a sequence of shots of Hamish in prison:
in the library;
in his cell alone;
in the canteen playing chess with a scary-looking inmate;
stared at by gangs as he passes by with his food on a tray.

More shots of spinning newspaper headlines – about his sentence, and a few about the lurid details of his affair, and the subsequent murder – and then a few other shots of the outside of the prison, including a clumsy series of time-lapse shots of a tree outside the prison losing its leaves and then coming into blossom.

We cut to Hamish being taken by the police in the back of a van to be transferred to another prison. They stop at traffic tights and he sees Eva with Miles Dawson in a restaurant. He catches their eyes.

We recognise the restaurant from the first scene.

He steals a gun off the policeman, bursts out of the car, and runs into the restaurant telling everyone else to leave.

He shoots Miles Dawson, then points the gun at Eva.

'I still don't know why you made me kill him. Why did you want him dead?'

'It was me and Miles who were having an affair. We were in love. But I was married. Married to his son, Ronnie. Me and Miles, we wanted to live better. We didn't want to be scraping around for crumbs any more. Miles fighting the bosses over clocking-in times, me drooled over every day by greasy businessmen who think a tea and a slice buys them a piece of me.'

'Why not just leave Ronnie?'

'Ronnie had a lot of money. The boxing business had made him a small fortune and if he found out I was leaving him for his father he wouldn't share any of it. And he was dangerous, violent. You know that. I decided the world would be a better place without him.'

'And Miriam? Who was Miriam?'

'The woman in the window? An actress. Good-time girl. We paid her to act as Miles's girlfriend to help him get a divorce.'

'And Mrs Dawson?'

'Miles's wife. Ronnie's mother. She's a good woman. A loving wife, a trusting wife. But sometimes that isn't good enough.'

'And you are her daughter-in-law.'

'Yes.'

'Nice.'

'Oh Hamish, I'm only trying to live, that's all, like everyone else in this hellhole. We are put here for a short time, we have to do something to make sense of it.'

'That neat trick with the drawing. I fell for that, didn't I?'

'You did.'

'How many twerps had you tried those sorts of tricks on before you found me?'

'A few. But none of them would have been right. I liked you, Hamish, loved you by the end. At the start, yes, it was all just to lure you in. But in the end I had feelings for you, those times we spent together were precious.'

'You evil…' Hamish pulls the trigger back.

'I'm not evil.'

'Then what?'

'It's not me that's evil. It's what I did.'

'But isn't that you?'

'I don't know. Who knows where badness comes from. Maybe it's just in you waiting to come out. Maybe it's in everyone. Or maybe it's just that some of us have the seed of it and something happens to us that nourishes and waters that black seed and then it grows and it flowers and all kinds of nastiness happens. Oh, I don't know, Hamish, who does?'

Shot of the gun barrel.

'Don't, Hamish, please. We could be good together. It would work for us. When you get out, I'll be waiting.'

The phone starts to ring and the camera zooms in on it and then tracks along the phone from the receiver to its coiled cord, until the coiled cord itself fills the screen for a few seconds, then in a devilishly clever leap of time, it pulls out to show Hamish's hand with the cord wound around it and pulls further out to reveal Hamish speaking on the phone to the policeman; we are back where the film started.

Hamish puts down the phone. The gun is still aimed at Eva.

Close-up on the trigger.

Close-up on his brow sweating. His finger trembling.

Close-up on Eva's face.

Close-up on Miles on the floor. He is not dead. He is lifting himself up quietly, slowly.

The camera starts to pull back and back, with no halt in its backward progress. It leaves the room and begins travelling down the corridor and out of the building to the police van outside.

Cut to the policeman in the van listening to the story on the phone. He puts down the phone and then we hear two shots from the restaurant.

The police are seen running towards the restaurant and the camera dollies back and then up high and then we see the scene from above.

Police storm inside. More shots are heard.

Silence.

A big wide shot of the city is followed by little smaller snippets of people in the city going about their business. Of the car plant at Longbridge and of people in the Hollow Egg, of people shopping at the rag market, of the church at St Martin's, of street traders at the Bull Ring, of people getting on and off buses, of people going in and out of cinemas. It's as if the camera is suddenly giving us a new view of the city, a superficial promotional film of the different public faces it offers to the world, oblivious to the subcultures of desire, transgression and crime that boil away beneath its surface.

Finally, the camera glides back to the restaurant. We see bodies coming out, covered in sheets, two of them, but we don't know who they are. Dawson and Eva? Hamish and Dawson? Eva and Hamish even?

The camera then dips low and crawls along the floor under the door and back into the restaurant.

It keeps going, on and on. It follows a line of blood

158

droplets on the lino until it reaches an open trap door into the drinks cellar. The camera swoops in. There is no music at this point, it's all in complete silence. We see a window which has been smashed and on the broken points of glass there is blood and a scrap of dark cloth from Eva's dress. We dive out of the dark cellar into blinding sunshine and for a few seconds the screen is whited out with glare, but then the exposure is adjusted and we see an empty sky with a few puffy clouds and for a short time the camera appears to be ascending into heaven. All is still silent at this point; there is no music or sound effects of any kind. Then, slowly fading up, we hear the tock-tock-tock of high heels on a pavement and then this fades out and is replaced by the creaking of wheels, the rattle and squeak of vehicle doors, low voices, and the camera dips to show two stretchers being put into the police van.

The words *The End* appear on the screen in wobbly white italics.

I ejected the cassette and pulled it out. I put it into its box and looked at the cover. I read the names on the back of everyone involved in making it but nothing rang a bell. I had watched every frame carefully, listened to every line of dialogue, and still I didn't have the answer.

I would have to start again from the beginning. I knew it was there somewhere. Fiona had been very clear.

CHAPTER SEVEN

1988

On the balcony I watched the traffic. Sometimes I liked to switch on the radio while I was out there and listen to the travel reports because they often mentioned this intersection. Radio 2 was best, although the music was dull. The announcer was a plummy posh girl who used nicknames for all the lorry drivers who phoned in – names like *eviltash* and *sunnymonkey* – as if she was a personal friend of all the truckers on the road. I wondered if signed pictures of her hung in their trucks and whether they masturbated about her. She mentioned this junction then – long delays on the M5 South today between Junctions 1 and 2 where a lane has been shut because of an incident involving a lorry, a coach and two motorbikes. I tried to imagine this accident and couldn't quite picture it. I couldn't help worrying about the two motorcyclists. Motorbikes look too vulnerable to be speeding along next to the giant mountains of metal that are trucks and coaches. The radio lady was right, I could see. Today it was such a long delay that drivers were getting out of their cars and walking about, talking to each other through the windows and smoking cigarettes. Some of them, the ones that I would call professional drivers, looked as though they were enjoying the break in their routine. It must be lonely, I thought, driving long distances for a living. You couldn't even pick up hitchhikers any more. I wondered whether there were special clothes you wore when you were a professional driver.

How many of Mathilde's fleet cars passed this way, heading towards the shops and supermarkets to sell their toffee?

I looked over towards the garages and wondered, like Mathilde, what John Ireland really wanted them all for. I never saw him opening one or closing one, putting anything in one, or taking anything out of one. I never saw him attend them to check that whatever was held inside them was safe, nor did he appear to have sublet them to anyone else.

I kept meaning to get him into conversation and see if I could find what he really wanted them all for, but apart from the time I saw him with his family in the paper shop, and the time he had found Mathilde and me trying to break in, he avoided me. If I noticed him in the park, watching the middle-aged women playing crown green bowls, he would move off when he saw me coming. If he was in the Frog and Railway, he would leave as soon as I entered. The only other person I'd ever seen near them was little Betty the other day when she emerged from behind them and then went off on her scooter.

Later that night Mathilde and I walked across the grassy area to where the garages were and stood over the road in front of the boarded-up arcade of shops, outside a defunct chip shop called the Happy Fryer. A peeling cartoon of a dancing fish with a big smile on its face was on the wall.

We watched from the shadows. Nothing happened for a

long time. Just the hum of traffic from the intersection and the low whoop of wind through the gap between the two blocks.

Mathilde was wearing a huge, bear-like coat and a trapper's hat with furry earflaps like she was in Russia or something. She had a leather hipflask with her which contained some kind of abrasive cherry-flavoured alcohol, and we kept swigging from it as we watched.

'What did you think about when you found out who I was?'

'I was worried, to be honest. I was worried that you might be like Eva Ni Riain. Evil. Like in the film.'

'Eva wasn't evil. She just did evil things. She wasn't a bad woman.'

'That's what you say in the film.'

'What *Eva* says.'

'She put poor Hamish in prison. She killed a man, she destroyed another's life, and she took the money and kept it.'

Near the garages there was a derelict bus shelter serving a bus route that didn't exist any more, and from behind it a skinny bedraggled fox, looking grey in the dim street lights, wandered into view and stared at us belligerently.

'Eva was a good woman at heart.'

'How is that?'

'All people are good inside. Some just do bad things. But that doesn't make them bad people, does it?'

'Well, it is sort of the dictionary definition. We are what we repeatedly do, someone said.'

The wind moved a plastic bag along the pavement in front of the garages, turning it over and over, making it look like a bird trying to take off.

'It's film noir, isn't it?' she went on. 'That thing you love.

It's always in the dark. They are always doing things in the dark and they can't always see properly what's going on. There are shadows. Shadows in the world and shadows in the head, and it is in these shadows that evil lurks.'

She passed me the hipflask and I took a long drink, the cherry flavour masking the stench of the alcohol.

A small car with no lights on moved slowly into view and stopped outside the garages. The driver switched off the engine but didn't get out. It looked like a man. There was a woollen hat and a thick coat. It could have been John Ireland, it could have been someone else, anyone. We saw him switch on the interior light for a moment and then off again, and then we saw smoke from a cigarette. The driver, whoever it was, seemed to be watching the garages like us.

'In the future,' Mathilde whispered, 'maybe scientists will have figured out how to turn evil back into good. Like turning fire into ice. Sometimes I think that an evil person needs to somehow live inside someone better, someone good. Find a good person and sort of occupy them. Like an inoculation against evil.'

'So we can all be good?'

'Maybe. Maybe, yes.'

I pulled on the hipflask again, the rough, sour liquid warming my throat briefly, but not much else.

The man in the small car started the engine and drove away, without putting on his lights.

Back on the balcony I looked at the sky. Even though we were in a big lit-up conurbation, you could still see a few stars, and I began to try and name them, as Fiona had taught me that night in Cumbria. Orion's Belt. The Plough. Arcturus. Cygnus. But I had no idea.

There were things about Fiona I should have noticed then, warning signs, changes that should have caused alarm. But I didn't put two and two together.

CHAPTER EIGHT

1987

We used to get bored in west Cumbria, and one Saturday
night we took a bus into the main town, Whitehaven, and
went drinking in the town centre pubs – the John Paul Jones,
the Dolphin, the Castle, the Chase Hotel. They were the
only ones really, and crowds of people would troop from one
to the other and back again all night long until they shut. We
had fun. We bumped into a few of my old school friends and
I introduced them to Fiona and we chatted about life away
from Cleator Moor, in the big city.

On Saturday nights the last bus home was 11 p.m. and
as last orders on Saturdays were also 11 p.m. we decided to
miss the last bus and instead have a few whiskies in Heapos,
a kind of disco bar, and walk back to Cleator Moor. It is
a long walk, well over an hour, up a huge steep hill out of
Whitehaven, and after that another big climb, way, way, way
up on to the moors where there is a long dark road with no
houses on it which takes you to Cleator Moor.

As we walked up Inkerman Terrace and out of Whitehaven we looked in the lit-up windows of the houses we
passed. We laughed at the lame pictures people hung on

their walls – clowns and yachts and tigers and horses and mountains – and the way people sat in their socks, feet upon stools, watching TV as if they were a million miles away from the real world, completely unaware that we were watching them from outside. We speculated why so many people didn't have curtains, and decided it must be a countryside thing; round here most people drove everywhere all the time and there would be very few people walking up this long hill out of town looking in at people through their windows.

We stopped to look at an old man and an old woman asleep in each other's arms as the light from the television flickered on their faces. Then we watched a man staring expressionlessly at the TV while he absently stroked his wife's head on his lap, as if she were a pet. Next door was a couple with a baby, and the man was walking up and down and rocking it to and fro while the girl watched TV over his shoulder, craning her head to the side every time he crossed her line of vision.

Once we were away from the houses there were only fields to look at and we walked through the blackness towards the town, which was lying there, lit up small and spangly in the shoulder of the black fells.

On this road the lack of pavements meant you had to be wary of passing traffic, because cars flew by at reckless speeds, usually drunks who had also been out on the town. We had to flatten ourselves into the hedge when an enthusiastic kid streaked by in a car full of his mates, and he was followed immediately by another, who overtook him on a blind bend then braked hard in front of him before accelerating off.

As we walked, Fiona pointed out the stars and told me what they were called.

'If you follow the curve of the Plough's handle you eventually get to Arcturus,' she said, 'which joins up the northern and southern sky. And from here, look, you can see the Milky Way! That shape like a flat spiral, see it? That bright band across the sky? And that over there,' she went on, 'is the Summer Triangle, which makes up the body of Cygnus, the swan.'

I said that I didn't care what they were called, I didn't want to know. I told her that I preferred the stars to exist as mere abstract shapes in the sky and said that for me the fact that the stars had names and constellations and were made of gas destroyed their mystery.

Fiona said that she couldn't believe this attitude and that knowledge and science only enhanced the pleasure you got from nature.

I said it didn't. I said that for me, sometimes, it destroyed it. I told her about someone once telling me that the sky wasn't really blue and explaining why it only *looked* blue, and I said that this had not improved my enjoyment of looking at a clear blue sky.

She said, well. I was really showing my small-town mentality now. She thought maybe I would also believe in intelligent design or something like that.

We began to argue quite hard about this subject, probably because we were drunk, and unusually for me, I really fought my corner because I felt that I was fighting for the romance of life and that she was fighting for the cold hard facts of banal existence.

'It's because you're a Catholic,' she said in the end. 'Catholics always revert to a superstitious way of looking at the world.'

'It is not,' I said. 'It fucking isn't.'

A car revved loudly in the distance behind and we took

the opportunity to take cover in the entrance to a field. It sped past, lighting up our faces momentarily and one of the lads in the car leaned out of the window and screamed 'fuckers' in a high voice. I worried that they would screech to a stop and reverse back, but they carried on up the road.

'I think that your attitude has a lot to do with the way you think about music as well,' I said to her.

'My attitude?' she said.

'You new composers. You see music as maths. Logarithms. A series of formulas you can manipulate. Sometimes it's like there's no love in the way you make music and that's why you need to know the name of everything and all about how everything works. That's why the music that you modern composers make sounds so cold.'

She went silent for a while. The distant hum of a car from somewhere. Then she climbed up on to the gate, jumped over into the field and walked away, calling back to me, 'Well if that's all you think of my music, then fuck you,' and she disappeared into the blackness.

I laughed. 'Hey, I'm sorry, come here, I was joking.'

But all I heard was her feet squelching in the mud around the side of the field and then I couldn't hear anything at all.

I became concerned. Fiona would have no idea where she was in relation to our house. She only knew the main roads. Negotiating a short cut like this across fields in the pitch dark would be impossible. I wouldn't even attempt it myself. I climbed the gate and set off along the side of the hedge, expecting her to jump out on me and say 'boo'. But nothing. After a time I found that the way was too muddy and treacherous with holes every now and again and unexpected tussocks of grass, and then a barbed wire fence blocked my way so I had to go back to the gate.

But back at the gate there was no sign of Fiona.

'Fiona,' I called into the darkness. 'Fiona, come on, I'm sorry. Stop joking about.'

Nothing but the soft wind.

I began to worry. There were slurry tips and random holes in the ground and old mine workings and abandoned farm machinery and all kinds of ways you could get into trouble. I listened harder. I could hear cows snuffling and snorting not far away and I remembered how a herd of cattle can turn on you if the beasts feel threatened. One of the cows lowed loudly and an owl hooted in the distance as if in response.

I tried again – 'Fiona, Fiona' – and then I began to run towards Cleator Moor to see if she had popped out further down the road at another entrance to the field, and was waiting for me there. But I got all the way to the edge of the town and there was no sign of her.

Now I began to panic. There was a phone box on the edge of the Mill Hill Estate and I wondered if I should call the police. I felt tears in my eyes at this point and I think it was then I realised that Fiona was a person I couldn't live without.

I ran and ran all the way to Crossfield Road where our house was and found the front door open.

Fiona was on the sofa in the front room watching motor-racing and drinking a glass of my dad's Lamb's Navy Rum. Her shoes and trouser legs were covered in mud, her jumper was splatted all over on the front, and her hair was sticking out at the sides, caked with brown splodges.

She didn't look at me. She drained her glass of rum with a deliberately loud slurp and topped it up from the bottle standing on the floor by her side. I noticed that she hadn't

bothered to mix it with anything despite there being miniature cans of Coke in the sideboard.

I sat next to her and placed my fingertips on the back of
her hand.

She returned the touch but kept looking ahead at the
Formula One cars screaming around the track.

Brazilian Grand Prix, the subtitle said next to a live broad-
cast symbol.

There were things about Fiona I should have noticed
even then. Changes in behaviour, in appearance even. Now
I thought back, her skin had begun to look different, her
eyes too, and she had been sleepy a lot of the time.

'I'm sorry,' I said.

'Me too,' she said.

'Life's too short.'

'Not for Catholics. You go on for ever.'

CHAPTER NINE

1988

I got home from my daily visit to the phone box (all was still progressing well up there in Cumbria) to find the thin-faced, long-nosed policeman in the spare room, flipping through a box of vinyl records while humming a jaunty tune.

'You sound happy.'

He turned and stared at me for a long time as if it was me who had entered his home uninvited rather than the other way round.

'Humming away there.'

'Cheerful and serious,' he said. 'I was told I had to be both at the same time in this job. This' – he held up the soundtrack to *A Clockwork Orange* – 'isn't this film banned? I heard it was violent. Do you like violence?'

'The music is mostly Beethoven and the violence in the film is highly stylised.'

'Which hurts the most – being punched for real or being punched in a stylised way?'

I took the album from him and replaced it in the box.

'What's this about, officer?'

'Do you mind if we sit down in your living room?'

I looked at my watch.

'Or do you call it a sitting room? I've always wondered what the difference was. The caretaker let me in, by the way.'

'I'll get the other chair off the balcony.'

'The home-constructed viewing platform. Yes. I remember that.'

Once we were settled into our seats, he leaned forward and spoke to me quietly as if the room were bugged.

'Little Betty again, I'm afraid.'

'Oh,' I said. My stomach tightened.

'She went off this afternoon and I'm sorry to say that she has not returned yet. It is now over eight hours and no word. As you can imagine, her mother is worried. But she has disappeared before and arrived home safely, so who knows.' His melodious voice seemed to infuse every fact with a heavy weight, as if each word was a lure to draw me into a sticky web he was weaving around me.

Betty gone again. I felt sick. Something about her when I saw her last week had seemed a little strange. The way she had appeared from behind the garages. But in truth I hadn't been worried. There was something purposeful and clever about Betty and the way she did things that made me confident in some way that she was OK, that she hadn't come to harm. In fact, I had began to wonder whether she had an alternative family, even, somewhere that she escaped to for a break from her disabled mother, someone she didn't want the authorities to know about. She always seemed so adult, so certain, never lost or confused.

'The last time she disappeared,' the policeman went on, 'you said you'd seen her from your balcony, didn't you?'

'I didn't see her from the balcony, no, not last time.'

'Oh. I thought you said you had.'

172

'Not last time, no.'

'Oh. But this time?'

'Well, I'm not sure. It depends when she was last seen.' A good reply, I thought, and wondered whether I was getting better at this.

'About noon today,' he said, and tilted his head back as if his peculiarly long nose were able to detect the motes of missing children on the air.

'I saw her last week. She went over towards the shops on her scooter.'

'Anything odd about her? Anything we should worry about?'

'She had a backpack with her, and a flask. I hadn't seen those before.'

'Oh.'

He took out his notebook and wrote this down.

'What do you think about Disney, Mr Quinn? Walt Disney.'

'I don't have an opinion.'

'Oh. You see, I understood from Miss Pelletier that you were a bit of a film buff.'

'Well, all I know is that Disney was in some ways a pioneer. The Russian film-makers were very influenced by him.'

'Dwarves keeping a woman captive in the forest? A boy made of wood who tells lies? Do you think they are wholesome tales for children?'

'Those are archetypal stories. Stories that reach right down into your soul. That's because they are about the things we all fear and the things we all desire.'

'Right. Fear and desire. You certainly don't talk like any of the other people I've interviewed around here, Mr Quinn. I mentioned Disney because I thought you might have noticed that Betty's backpack had a patch sewn on to it that referred to a Disney film called *Flight of the Navigator*. I wondered if it was somehow relevant? You with your knowledge of films?'

'I have never seen that film,' I said. 'But I know she likes it because she always says, "See you later, navigator." I couldn't see the details of the patch on her bag from up here.'

He leaned back and looked at the ceiling while he thought about this. 'It seems that you, Mr Quinn, see some things clearly, but you don't see others. Very selective. Have you ever had your head looked at?'

'Do you mean has anyone ever looked at my head? Well, yes, I guess everyone who meets me looks at my head, in the way that they look at every part of me.'

'You think that people look at every part of you?'

'Yes, I expect they do. I know I look at every part of people I meet.'

'You look at every part of a person? Isn't that a little uncomfortable for people? Have you looked at every part of me?'

I shook my head and smiled.

'You smile. Some people have a winning smile that can help them get away with anything. Lovable rogues, we call them. You're not one of them, I'm afraid. Your smile makes you look more shifty, Mr Quinn. The truth is, we have people who can have a look at your head, if needs be. They can have a look at what's going on inside it and they can find out an awful lot about someone. I don't know how they do it, I just trust them.'

'Have they ever looked at your head?' I said.

'Ah, yes, interesting – who examines the examiners? We had a module about that at police college. But I was off sick on that day. One of those really bad colds when everything seems echoey and it's like you're inside a thick blanket.' He rubbed the end of his long nose as if remembering the feeling of having that cold.

'So, I never found out who examines the examiners. You didn't mention to anyone about seeing her last week? Little Betty?'

'No. I supposed she was just going down the shops.'

'With a rucksack and a flask.'

'Yes'

'Mmm,' he said, and fell silent for a time. Then he took out his notebook and began scribbling in it. He looked about the room again, his eyes crawling over every surface like the lens of a photocopier.

'What's that?' he said, jumping up and bounding over to the wall. It was the round patches of dark mould, and he stared at these stains intently, as if they were the ghostly imprints of some mysterious event.

'Condensation,' I said.

He looked to his side for a source of information that wasn't there.

'Warm air meeting a cold surface,' he said, as if recording his words on an invisible device. 'But,' he turned to me, 'what makes the air warm and what makes the walls cold?'

'I'm no scientist,' I said.

'That's a shame,' he said. 'Because when civilisation breaks down, people like me, the people who understand maths and science, will rule and you will be our slave. I'll be back in touch, Mr Quinn. But if anything occurs to you that you might have forgotten to tell me, please do just give me a ring,' and he held out a business card which I took and shoved into my back pocket.

At the door he took out his notebook again. 'Just one more question. If you were forced to describe yourself as something, what would you say you were? Your job, I mean. Your profession.'

'It depends who was forcing me, why they were forcing me, and what means of force they were using.'

He smiled. 'I'll put unemployed.'

CHAPTER TEN

1988

Later, I couldn't sleep so I sat on the balcony with a blanket to keep me warm and as the night moved into the small hours I watched the traffic, the white and red lights floating over the concrete lanes.

It was 3.30 a.m. when the letterbox rattled and I knew it wasn't little Betty.

Mathilde couldn't sleep either. She needed company. We believed at the time that it was because we were both worrying about Betty; but in truth, I think it was something else drawing us together.

I went to get whisky and when I returned she was standing motionless in the middle of the room, staring. It was as if she could see the ghosts of Hamish McGrath and Otto the director and the script girls and the best boy and the gaffer and the lighting men and sound men flitting about the room going about their work, imprinted into the fabric of the walls like a Victorian lantern show. She was hypnotised and I followed her gaze and after a time believed that I too could make out some faint shadows that might have been the spectral remnants of that powerful story.

We took our drinks on to the balcony, even though it was freezing, and I wondered whether she would share my pleasure in watching the motorway intersection, but although she watched with me for a few moments, the long kiss she planted hard on my lips took my mind off matters relating to traffic flow around the West Midlands transport infrastructure. When the kiss stopped she curled her arm around my back and we stood side by side looking out into the dark night.

I was going to speak. I was going to say, no this is not right, it's really not the right time for me, and, in honesty, that's what I was thinking. Yes, I was feeling desire for this woman, this woman I had so often watched on screen and fantasised about. I felt a kind of urgent, persistent lust which was beginning to absorb me completely, and make me feel that unless I spent this lust right here, right now, it might disappear and never present itself again. But the power of the recent events and the thought of Fiona, who I was still deeply, fully, completely entangled with in every aspect of my existence, pulled my thoughts away from sex with this beautiful fading film star.

'Why don't you come away with me?' she said.

'Where to?'

'Rue Daguerre in Montparnasse. *Paree*. Remember, I told you about it. The cafés, the cheese shops, the bakeries, the jazz clubs, the little cinema with the American crime films. All the things I told you about. I have that little flat there still.'

'The graves of the existentialists where there aren't any flowers.'

'Yes. You will come, won't you?'

'I have some issues in Cumbria.'

She looked up at the sky for a time then down to the

floor, then back at me, as if she was recalibrating something in her head.

'Then you have a pause in your life,' she said. 'A natural pause that will help you and me. It will help us see things more clearly. It's not often life offers you a pause. It's as if everything is frozen and you are able to walk about and look at things, study things, work out whether you are doing it right, whether your life is in the right place. Maybe this is a pause you have been offered for a reason.'

'I'm not sure,' I said.

'You will come,' she said.

'I'm not sure,' I said.

'Don't think about it. Thought is the enemy of action. You must come. You will come. Eventually we will both be there.'

All things move towards their end and that's when I saw it. Rather than wait for the slow grumbling lift we ran down the stairs, me counting down the levels in my head as I always did, 7, 6, 5, 4, 3, 2, 1, and looking out of the dark windows at each level, to check that nothing had changed.

I was hyper-aware of the sound of my footsteps in the echoing footwells which seemed louder and more clattering than usual.

When we got outside there were hard winds and the street lights around the grassy area were shaking. A flurry of thin snow whirled against the tops of the two blocks of flats. We waited in the shadows. It was cold and there was no one else about. A low mist hung across the grassy area and everywhere was silent.

'What did you see?' Mathilde said quietly.

'A movement, a light. Maybe the door of one of the garages opening.'

We looked towards the row of eight garages and waited. If this was film noir I could guess the plot. John Ireland would be her evil ex-husband and Mathilde would arrange it so I would murder him. Mathilde would get his money, run off with her new boyfriend, and I would go to prison. That was the usual way.

We stood close together, our hips touching. Her breath, when she turned to look in my direction, was warm on my cheek.

Behind us, high up on the motorway intersection, red and white lights poured through the black.

Then I saw it again.

A hem of light from under one of the garage doors.

We walked over to the door in question. We could hear someone moving about inside, a clink of metal. A car door creaked open and then clunked shut. Then the same sound again. The rustle of something. It was hard to hear properly with the rumble of the motorway so close.

Dread crept through me. I looked at the hem of light under the door. And then at one end, a section of the light disappeared. Then another block of light went and we could make out that someone was using pieces of cloth to block the opening at the bottom of the door. A few more pieces of cloth were jammed under the door until no more light could be seen. The creak of a car door again, then the tinkle of keys, then the rush of an engine followed by a dull rolling sound as it turned over quietly. We looked at each other and Mathilde banged her fist on the door. But nothing happened.

'Wait there,' she said, and I watched as she ran back towards the block of flats, her tall, slim figure quickly disappearing into the mist.

I banged hard on the garage door and this time I shouted too. 'Hey, hey, hey.' I began to feel very, very frightened. I didn't really know how long something like that would take. I thought about the day I had met his wife and children in the paper shop. But it might not be John Ireland in there. It might be someone else. Or John Ireland might be doing something to someone else. In that case should I stay, or should I run? The red and white lights on the motorway intersection seemed slower and larger than normal, heavy ponderous blobs floating past in a misty chain. It was as if the lights were more connected than usual, as if the line of traffic was one long, vulnerable creature crawling to a safe destination so it could get some sleep.

Mathilde appeared at my side with the screwdriver she'd used last time and prised open the door with one quick movement. The space smelt horribly of petrol fumes. We found a light and switched it on. The garage was completely empty, but for the car. No tools, no chairs, no ladders, nothing. A tube from the exhaust pipe went through the back window of the car to where John Ireland was lying on the back seat. His eyes were closed and his skin looked sweaty. His hands were formed into fists that clutched at the cuffs of his jumper. Jangling electric guitars were playing from the radio. A bottle of vodka with a few inches left in it was lying on its side next to him. A plastic bag on the back seat had a Sony Walkman in it with a handwritten sticker on its side that said *listen*.

I slid the Walkman into my coat pocket.

Mathilde leaned into the driver's side and clicked the ignition key to off. I pulled the hose pipe off the exhaust. I opened the back door of the car and shook John Ireland hard. He slurred some words at me, moved his head from side to side, and raised his hands. The fumes were so powerful I thought that I might pass out. My head began to feel as though it were emptying of something, and my fingers and toes began to tingle.

We managed to drag him out and sat him against the neighbouring garage door, slapping his face to keep him awake.

'Should I run to the phone box?' I said.

'Be quicker if we take him ourselves,' Mathilde said.

She went back into the garage and I heard the ignition firing and the engine stuttering and stalling. And then she ran back over. 'I think he's flooded it.'

Then I saw Mathilde's eyes alight on an old Vauxhall parked at the bottom of the flats and we left John lolling against the garage door and ran towards it. Mathilde prised the driver's door open as if she'd done this sort of thing many times before, jumped into the driver's seat, jammed the screwdriver into the ignition, and started it. I never knew that stealing a car would be so easy.

After we had bundled John into the back seat Mathilde threw the car into gear and we roared off towards the M6 slip road. Once we were on the motorway I felt a rush of excitement. I was in the very place I spent my time watching. From here I could see my own flat, the lights still on, the balcony door still open. I could even make out a twinkle of reflected light from the two glasses of whisky standing on the balcony rail. Mathilde threw the car into neutral, accelerated loudly, then changed down a gear to get more thrust, and used the inside lane to scream past a truck that was tootling along down the middle before swerving in front of it dangerously to get into the fast lane. Then she rocketed away at over ninety towards our exit.

I was in a stolen car being driven dangerously at high speed by a femme fatale from the movies, and we were on our way to save a man's life. How did Mathilde know how to steal a car? The edges of the entertainment world seemed to overlap with the edges of the criminal world in a way I had never considered before. Mathilde concentrated on propelling the car as fast as she could towards help. John Ireland was making a low moaning noise in the back and I leaned back and shook him to keep him awake, having a vague idea that if we allowed him to sleep he might never wake up again. When we got to our junction she had to swerve the car across all three lanes of traffic to get on to the slip road, but she did it easily, seemingly without thinking, horns going off behind her as several cars had to change lanes or brake to allow us through.

John Ireland's wife was summoned and after she'd been with her husband on the ward for a while, she came and sat with us in the waiting area. She looked pale and her hands were shaking. She stared at everything with an intense expression as if she were trying to make sense of an upside-down map of somewhere she knew well. Her face still bore the trace of that smile, that smile she always had.

'So glad we got there when we did,' said Mathilde.

Mrs Ireland said nothing for a time, just looked about her at the room. She picked up and put down a magazine.

Then she said, 'John and I met at Walsall Tech when we were teenagers and neither of us has ever been with anyone else. Whenever I saw him with people from work he was always laughing. And with the children. He laughed all the time. It turns out that I never knew him. I suppose it was all a mask. They say he'll be OK. They say there won't be any side effects.'

'Sometimes you just can't see a way around things,' Mathilde said. 'You can't get past them. And they get bigger and bigger and they seem to black you out. I've had it. It's like a giant version of yourself, ten times your weight, crushing you.'

John's wife turned to me. 'John said he liked you. "That last fella whose garage I got? I like him," he said.'

'John is a big man,' I said. 'A big man inside and a big man outside. He'll get through it.'

'Did you ever wonder why he wanted all the garages?'

'I just thought he was one of those people who liked things to be complete.'

'John had this very particular view about life and the world. He thought that life was too busy and that every space was always too full of objects and clutter and people's possessions. Not long after we'd met he told me that one day he'd like to own a space with absolutely nothing in it. Once he owned a space with nothing in it he would be happy. So when we moved here he rented one of the garages and kept it completely empty. And it made him happy. But then he wanted more, and that's when he started getting the rest of them, until he had the whole row. The more empty garages he owned, the happier he was. He said that it relaxed him. At night, if he couldn't sleep, all he had to do was think of that row of empty garages and he would drift off like a baby. After he'd rented the last garage in that row, your garage, he started thinking about renting garages in other streets and even other towns, and keeping them all empty. "Imagine that," he used to say. "Imagine garages all over the country, even all over the world, all with nothing in them but empty space. What a wonderful thing that would be." Oh, I love him so much,' she said and then she started to cry, and I put my hand on her arm.

*

Back at my flat, I lay on the mattress feeling the underfloor heating pulsing through my body. My life in the last few weeks had been too busy, too full of incident. I wanted to exist for a time like a basic animal would. To look at the colour and the shape and the weight of things around me but not think about the relationship of things to each other. Feel the geography of the place I am in but not think about other geographies, other places I might be. Hear the sounds of people talking but not the words. Hear the sound of traffic moving but not think about where it is going. Smell the cooking of food but not think about who is cooking it for whom.

I thought about the empty garage. I thought about the walls, the plain bare walls. I thought about the inside of the door, blank from edge to edge in all four directions. I thought about the dark corners with nothing in them but balls of dust, and I thought about the bare ceiling and the bare floor.

CHAPTER ELEVEN

1988

The next morning the letterbox flapped making my heart jump and when I opened the door and saw a familiar figure – the long grey hair, the ring in her nose, the motorcycle boots – I knew that Betty would be at her side again as she had been last time.

And there she was. Safe.

'I had another of my days out, Mr Quinn. I'm sorry that I upset everyone again. But sometimes it gets like I'm in prison down there.'

This time we went inside my flat because Betty had a lot to say about her recent escapade.

'I love my mother and wouldn't want anyone else to look after her. But as I'm only twelve I sometimes think I might be missing out on life. In my favourite film, *Flight of the Navigator*, Max, the robot that drives the spaceship, says we only use 10 per cent of our brains. So when I am given a task by my mother – any simple task, like cleaning the grill or going to post a letter – I think, how can I make this errand more complicated, more interesting? How can I make this job really fill my day, and use up more of my thinking power? So what happened was this: my mother asked me to go and buy some knives and forks because I keep putting them in the bin by mistake when I am washing up. But she didn't know where to get them and I didn't either so I said I would go out and investigate. I went to the library and a book there said that the main manufacturing town in England for knives and forks was a city called Sheffield – have you heard of it?'

'Yes,' I said.

'So I found out that there was a train to Sheffield from Birmingham that only took an hour and so I went there because I knew I could definitely get knives and forks there, if anywhere, and I did, I found some in a big shop called De-benhams. After that I had some time left – or so I thought – so I went for a walk around to explore the place and I ended up scooting down to a housing estate a bit like this one. And I got a bit lost. And then it got late. And I knew I had missed the train I was supposed to get and I didn't know the times of the others so I found a phone box and rang the station and that's when I found out all the trains were cancelled. An overhead power lines failure. No trains till the following day, the man said. And by then it was cold and dark. So I thought, well, I will have to just find somewhere safe to sleep until it gets light and then I can find my way back and the trains will be working again. And I was wandering about near this big estate looking for a shed or garage or something I could hide in, when a nice man appeared. He said that he was a construction worker and he was building the biggest shopping centre in Europe. It was called Meadowland and I liked the sound of it. It sounded like something out of a film. He said he had seen me from up in his crane, with his binoculars. Was I OK? Did I need a lift somewhere? Or was there someone he could ring up for me? I said no. I said that if he rang anyone official then my mother would be in big trouble because she needs me to care for her. We can't have the social workers taking me away from her because then who would look after her? Some paid lackey who'd treat her like meat? And he agreed. It was better that families stayed together. But I said I really did need somewhere to stay, and he said, well, if that's all I needed, the safest place to stay would be in the cabin of his crane. And he pointed up and there it was, lit up against the black sky, a giant thing like a metal dinosaur with a glass bubble on top. He said it had a bed in it and everything, and I could stay in it as long as I was out by seven o'clock the next morning. I would be in the safest place in the world up there, he said, no one ever thinks about climbing up a crane on a building site.'

As she described all this to us her voice remained still, calm and clear, as if she were telling us about a routine trip to the local shop.

'We had to go over a bridge across a river to get to this crane and when I stood at the bottom looking up at it I couldn't believe I would be able to climb it. But I did. He helped me. It was a long climb, really high and very exciting, like going up the beanstalk, but it felt safe because there is a metal cage all around you as you climb up, and there's a place halfway where you can have a rest. This man, the crane man, he was really panting by then, even though he must have done the climb himself every day. His name was Gareth, by the way, Gareth Close. When I got to the top I couldn't believe the view. You could see all over the city. He pointed out where I had been when he spotted me, and showed me the binoculars he used to help him see what was going on on the ground. He said that I had seemed very lost and out of place. I looked out of the cabin and it was like looking down on Polly Pocket Land. Even though it was dark, you could make out loads of tiny lit-up boxes, which were houses, and things that looked like twisting rivers, which were roads, and you could see the lights of tiny cars crawling along like microbes. He showed me how I could sleep on this sofa thing and there was an electric lamp and he showed me how it worked and he said I should get up at 6.30 and go down and then go to the railway station. He left me some crisps and a sandwich and a ten pound note in case I needed breakfast in the morning and then he went off and left me.'

I turned to the social worker and the look on my face must have been one of horror.

'Mr Quinn,' she said, 'I know what you are thinking and we were all thinking the same thing. But this all checks out and Mr Close, the crane operator, Gareth, he has been interviewed by the police and it turns out he was just helping out. There was no intent to do any harm at all. So it looks as though not every stranger who meets a child is a murderer.'

When they had gone, I went to my jacket and took out the Sony Walkman John Ireland had left in the car. I opened it and extracted the cassette. A C30, spooled halfway in. About five minutes of sound recorded by the looks of it. I didn't think it would be right to give this tape to Mrs Ireland. I thought about her face with its perpetual smile and the tears that would run down it if she sat down with the headphones and listened to John Ireland's rumbling voice describing whatever problems he'd been having. And I imagined him sitting opposite her while she listened to this macabre recording, his head in his hands as he wished she had never come across it.

I found a pencil and with its sharpened point teased out a curl of tape. Then I tugged it all out of the cassette, every little inch, clump after clump of it, until it was a spaghetti of brown on the floor, like a pile of intestines. I stuffed the cassette and the yards of brown tape into my bin, the tape spilling out over the edge, and went to the bedroom. I picked up the *Out of the Dark* soundtrack cassette Fiona had made for me, put it into the Walkman, lay back on the bed, and pressed play. I had never listened to this recording before on headphones and the experience was very revealing. I could hear so much more detail. It came to the scene where Hamish is roaming the streets alone, terrified of being arrested, and he is standing outside a random house, looking in through the window at a children's birthday party. The throbbing dissonant music on the soundtrack is blending with the children singing 'Happy Birthday' out of tune. The 'Happy Birthday' song itself is almost completely drowned out by the thick, droning, dissonant strings, and deep brass stabs of Penderecki's soundtrack, a noise which so well represents Hamish's mind at the time. But unlike when you watched it on the video, using the headphones there were certain points when the score dips out a little so that the jolliness of the tune can contrast with the hideous cacophony of the music, and you could hear the singing much more clearly. And it is this:

Happy birthday, dear Katya

A strange name but a beautiful one. Apparently, it was the actual name of Otto Schneider's daughter, and, if I remembered correctly, the child actress in the scene was his actual daughter and it was her real birthday party that they filmed.

I stopped the tape and thought about the blissfully happy expression on the child's face. On Katya's face. Katya.

My job was done.

I packed a few things into a rucksack, left the flat, and took a 51 to Digbeth coach station. I got on the 13.26 to Cumbria and sat there looking out of the window as we rolled through Birmingham towards the M6 and the north.

CHAPTER TWELVE

1987

After the night of the big argument, there were no more late drinks in Whitehaven and no more long walks back on deserted roads in the dark. Because it was not long after that that Fiona began to get the headaches and started to spend a lot of time in bed. Sometimes she felt as though she was swelling up and about to explode. We had been in Cumbria for three months by then and it was nearly Christmas. The days started to blur into each other, each day more grey and murky than the last, a series of nondescript days where it wasn't cold, it wasn't warm, and the weather didn't even seem to be there. And because there was nothing to do – no appointments and no work for either of us – the days went quickly, running together into each other, and became like one day lived concurrently with the others.

Fiona had consulted the big old-fashioned medical book my parents kept on the shelf. I knew that particular volume well. I would often frighten myself as a child by looking at it, with its crude line drawings of people with lockjaw and people having cysts lanced into bowls, and its stories about people hiccuping for thirty years. But it didn't hold the secret to what was causing Fiona's ailments.

The coach was heading out of the city and on to the motorway and it wasn't long before I was passing the flats on the Yew Tree. Number 69, Acacia Avenue. I wondered what John Ireland would be doing, and whether he would keep all his garages. Maybe he was watching the motorway now from his window in the other block. I waved out of the coach window.

In west Cumbria, we had been living in a limbo land where everything had been suspended. Reality seemed slower, and things less real, as if we were preserved in jelly.

We watched a lot of television. *The Singing Detective* was on and I remember when Fiona wasn't feeling so ill, we would dance together to the funny old songs, cavorting faster and faster until we fell on to the sofa, laughing.

The bus stopped in the main street at Kendal. Outside a café, a middle-aged man with a screwed-up red face was holding a long piece of wood.

That final night in Cleator Moor I was lying next to Fiona on the bed in the attic upstairs, listening to her breathing as she snoozed. I sat up and leaned my chin on my hand and looked at her closely. Her face seemed puffy and swollen. In fact, she had said a few days earlier that she thought her eyes, her actual eyeballs, had changed shape, so that her contact lenses didn't fit any more and she had gone back to her glasses. She had so many different obscure health problems by that point that she had begun to joke that all of these things were caused by Cumbria in some way. Must be the Cumbrian water, she would say. Or this Cumbrian air. Or the dampness from all those lakes. Or the mountains casting cold shadows over everything. Or the pollution from

Sellafield nuclear plant. Or the Marchon chemical works on the coast. Or even the old open-cast iron ore mines putting floaty spores of metal into the air.

Fiona's book was lying open on her chest where it had fallen. *The Unbearable Lightness of Being*, by Milan Kundera. Two pages in, as she had been for weeks. Reading and listening to the radio at the same time was a thing we both liked to do. The storage heater was blasting out, making the room like a greenhouse. The heat and Radio 4 seemed like part of the same system, soothing waves of comfort we luxuriated in together like a warm bath.

Fiona snored loudly and turned over. Her brow was covered in slick sweat, her dark hair sticking to it, and I went to the bathroom and got a flannel and ran it under the cold tap with the idea that I could maybe hold it against her forehead. But then I didn't because I worried it would wake her up. I wondered whether I should take her temperature. But I was sure it would be fine. Anyway, it was extremely warm in there with the storage heater on full, and I remembered we didn't have a thermometer in the house. Fiona had an appointment at the doctor's the next day so I was sure it would be all sorted then.

The coach pulled in at Keswick bus station. A tall man with a Paul Weller-type feather cut and a Harrington jacket was standing at a stop talking to an old woman.

I lay down next to Fiona and tried to stop worrying. I concentrated on the report on the World Service, about Eastern Europe and the Velvet Revolution. The Iron Curtain was melting away. Romania, Czechoslovakia, Poland, everywhere. No one knew what was going to happen with East and West Germany. The screws were rattling in the machine and the East was falling apart, or rather falling together again in some people's opinion. Countries that I had never heard of were mentioned all through the night: Lithuania, Georgia, Belarus, Kurdistan.

The coach was coming into Cockermouth and we paused at some traffic lights outside a children's nursery. Some boys in a sandpit were using plastic spades as guns, going *chew chew chew*.

Chew chew chew.

Chew chew chew.

Minutes after my father had rung 999 I heard the siren sounding from a long way off and I looked out of the attic window and saw the ambulance moving towards us a couple of miles away, its flashing lights clearly visible on the long dark road from Whitehaven to Cleator Moor.

I sat on the floor next to where Fiona lay and held her head in my arms. I seemed to float out of myself and looked down from the ceiling on to a tableau of me and Fiona on the floor, me holding Fiona's head on my lap.

She was conscious again now and her breathing was OK, but her body was quivering, and if I asked her anything, her answers were slow, slurry and confused.

I heard the ambulance coming down Crossfield Road, its low diesel rumble, and heard the creak of its handbrake, the door clattering open, the squeak of hinges, and then wheels rolling on the pavement, and the tense voices of my parents.

Lights came on in a house opposite and people came out to look.

An ambulanceman burst into the attic bedroom carrying boxes full of tubes and wires, and he was followed by another man with a stretcher.

The lead ambulanceman was short and squat with a ruddy face and he grinned and called out, 'What's tha bin dayin', love?' in a thick west Cumbrian accent. He knelt next to her, put his hand on her throat, and looked to the side. His lips moved as he appeared to be counting. He motioned with his head to the other ambulanceman, the way footballers communicate to players across a field, and the other man opened his box and attached a blood-pressure cuff to Fiona's upper arm.

'Fiona,' he said into her face. 'Fiona, we're going to have to take you into hospital. Don't worry, you'll be all right.'

'Has she taken anything?' the other one asked me.

'No. I don't think so,' I said. 'But she's been having headaches over the last few days.'

'OK,' said the ambulanceman. 'Headaches. And has she told the doctor?'

'She has an appointment tomorrow.'

He got out a stethoscope and listened to her stomach then made a quizzical face.

The other man gave her an injection of something into her arm.

Fiona stared at the men, smiling faintly, the way you might at a harmless mad person.

The men got her on to the stretcher, soothing and encouraging her with cheerful jokes and endearments, and got her down the two flights of stairs quickly.

Outside the sun was just beginning to peep over the horizon.

I climbed into the back of the ambulance and sat next to Fiona and held her hand. The injection she had been given seemed to have made her drowsy and although she spoke to me as we went along, nothing she said made any sense. She seemed to be speaking from another world, a world of fluffiness and wooziness where everything had soft edges.

196

When we got to casualty, medical staff were waiting for us and they helped unload the trolley and wheeled Fiona into a room which seemed to have been set out ready for her. In the room a young, floppy-haired doctor with a soft, glowing, hairless face examined her carefully and fitted her up to a monitoring machine. He put a cannula in her wrist and set up a drip for drugs. He was concentrating so hard on the job in hand he didn't seem to notice me standing there. He gave short, softly spoken instructions to the nurses who darted about getting things and switching things on and off. They put a tube into her mouth and linked her to a breathing machine which made shushing and hissing noises.

Then the young blond doctor went into a corner and changed from his trainers into white wellington boots.

An older man appeared, and a nurse in a dark blue uniform.

There was a short period while the older man and the young doctor and the nurses stood in a corner and said things to each other in low voices.

Then the young blond doctor called me over.

'We are going to have to get the baby out.'

I sat down on the floor and closed my eyes.

'It's very early, three months early, we think. But viable. Absolutely viable, nowadays. We have an excellent neonatal unit in Carlisle. The baby will be sent there by air ambulance right away.'

I opened my eyes. 'What's neonatal?'

'It's in Carlisle,' he said. 'It's where the baby will be best looked after.'

'Carlisle is a long way away.'

'Fiona will need constant monitoring after the baby has been removed.'

'I don't have a car.'

'There's some forms. Someone will go through them with you.'

'If there is a baby, Fiona will want to be near it. The baby.'

'I understand you're upset,' said the doctor. 'We are going to do the best for the baby and your wife. *Maureen*,' he called out to a nurse nearby, 'could you take Mr Quinn to the waiting room and get him some tea?'

I looked towards Fiona where she lay surrounded by staff making quick, precise preparations around her and I went across, put my mouth to her ear and sang 'Cruising Down the River'.

I was put in a waiting room with no windows. There was no one else in there. My parents must have been sent somewhere else to wait. They would be wondering what was happening, but I couldn't contact them and didn't want to move from this room because this was where the doctors knew I was.

A massive clock dominated the wall and its click seemed to get louder with each second like a giant bird pecking a steel pipe. Its hands said ten to eleven. We had been there over three hours. I sat down and flicked through some magazines. *Practical Boat Owner*, *What Car?* One about gardening, one about fish-keeping, one about horses too.

I was worried about the hospital forms they'd said I had to fill in. What if I filled them in wrongly and ticked all the wrong boxes against all the wrong things? I was twenty-five and just didn't feel old enough to take all this on.

I had noticed a payphone outside in the corridor and after finding some ten pence pieces I went out there. I called Fiona's mother. She answered right away but at first she didn't understand who I was, as I had never rung her before, and she kept thinking it was a different Daniel, a Daniel she had round to do her decorating.

'Sorry, Danny, I don't think I called you about anything recently, did I?' she said. 'Did you leave something here? Or is there a bill I should have paid?'

'No. I'm the other one, the other Daniel,' I said. 'Fiona's boyfriend.'

There was a long pause, and then she said, 'Where's Fiona?'

'Fiona isn't all right,' I said.

Just as I had put down the phone, the doctor appeared.

'You can come and see your daughter now,' he said, beaming all over his face.

I followed him down some corridors and he bustled me into a side room, and there she was, a tiny quivering sliver of pink flesh lying on a white sheet. Her face was scrunched up and red and she was whimpering and shaking. Her skin was smeared in a grey, furry substance like grease.

'Pick her up. Hold her,' the doctor said, 'it's OK,' and the nurse wrapped the baby in a white blanket and handed her to me.

I looked down at her for a long time, her little eyes squeezed shut, her tiny mouth sipping at the air.

Tears came.

'She looks like a strong little thing. A fighter,' the doctor said. 'We are going to ventilate her and then we need to move her to Carlisle where they have all the best staff and equipment.'

'A girl,' I said.

'Yes. Do you have a name?'

'Yes. There's a name Fiona likes. She once said that if

199

she ever had a baby and if it was a girl, she knew what she would call it. But I don't know what it is.'

'I'll write Baby Quinn on a wristband for now. Let's go and introduce baby to her mother.'

Fiona was awake but drugged and slurry and when I held the little baby up to her face and said, 'Look. We have a little baby,' she smiled a little, as much as she could with the ventilation tube in her mouth. 'What was the girl's name you said you liked? Remember when you were watching *Out of the Dark* and you said there was a name in the film that you liked and that if you ever had a little girl that's what you would call her?'

Fiona couldn't answer.

Then something seemed to come to rest within her and she sank deeper into her pillows and closed her eyes as though she knew that a large task had been completed and that she could now rest and recover.

I was taken away to watch them prepare the baby for the air ambulance. The nurse weighed her and wrote down a number. Two pounds something, I seem to remember, about the same size as a bag of sugar. I didn't know what babies were supposed to weigh but I knew this was small. They put a ventilator tube into her mouth and put her in an incubator on wheels that reminded me of a hostess trolley.

The nurse who had been allocated to her was called Theresa Fleming. Her face seemed always creased up in a big smile, her eyes little slots with laughter lines shooting out at the sides. She looked as ecstatic as if the baby were her own and she spoke breathlessly and quickly as if everything was urgent and special and, as she spoke, tears were always welling at the corners of her eyes.

'A baby of that size will normally be in hospital for a

month or two at least so we can get some weight on her and make sure she's healthy and fit. We are all so happy we got her out safely. She won't be on the ventilator long,' the nurse explained. 'We keep reducing the strength of the ventilator until she's breathing on her own and then we take it away. But she'll need to be in oxygen-enriched air, so we have a little box, a little see-through box like this' – she held one up – 'and we put that over her head and there's a pipe goes in here, with oxygen flowing through, and we take some blood every hour, from her heel, just a little tiny pinprick, to see how well she is absorbing it and then we adjust the oxygen levels accordingly so we don't cause any damage. See that dial at the bottom of the see-through box? That tells you the percentage of oxygen in the air and it should always correspond to the number written on the end of the incubator, which will change with each blood test. If you're here, let us know if the reading goes up higher than it should and we can turn the oxygen level down.'

There was a large TV on wheels that was attached to the incubator and showed lots of readings and levels and made beeps and bloops as well. The baby was lying on what the nurse called an apnoea mat which sounded an alarm if she stopped breathing.

I wished I could become as small as the baby and sleep in a little cot next to it in the incubator.

'You can ring them at the neonatal unit in Carlisle at any time,' she said, 'and they will tell you how your little baby is doing. You can visit any time of day as well and stay as long as you want. There's even a room with a bed if you want to sleep there in Carlisle near your baby. Look,' she said and handed me an instant Polaroid they had taken of the baby. 'That's for you. That's your little girl. Look. She's so lovely, isn't she? You can show this to Mum when she comes round. Mum will be groggy for a day or so, but show her that picture and you can tell her all about her baby. In a few days we'll be able to move Mum to Carlisle too so they can be together.'

In the next few hours Fiona's mum and dad arrived. Her mother was in tears but her father was as still and silent as if he was concussed. He kept asking the staff what he could do to help and looked desperate to be given some sort of job, so one of the nurses sent him down to the café to get drinks for everyone and he took on this task with relish.

Nurse Fleming had been assigned to sit at Fiona's side continuously. Every fifteen minutes a blood-pressure cuff around her upper arm pumped itself up automatically, and a new reading appeared on the screen and Nurse Fleming checked it and wrote it down on a chart.

She talked to Fiona kindly as if she were looking after a small child.

You're doing great, pet.
You're doing so fine, pet.
You're doing just perfect, pet.

Every couple of hours a doctor appeared and did a few extra checks. The worrying thing was that Fiona showed no sign of coming out of her state of unconsciousness. She was still breathing heavily with the help of the ventilator tube and she looked hot and slick with sweat. The doctor said not to worry unduly. It was the body's way of recovering from a trauma, he said. Sometimes the patient will be out for a good while, and the drugs they have given her will also keep her drowsy. We need to get her blood pressure down, that's the main thing, he said. Once we have that under control we can start to bring her round, bring her back to reality. She is in no discomfort, he assured us. She is just sleeping and dreaming away there. In a world of her own, he added, in a kind of wistful way as if he himself wished he could be in a drug-induced coma for a few days.

There were decisions to make, decisions to be made right away. Who should stay with Fiona, and who should go to Carlisle to be with the baby?

But these decisions didn't need to be taken.

Because as hard as they tried, and they really did try, the doctors were unable to keep Fiona alive.

I drove round the one-way system over and over again for what must have been an hour. Then I swung down to the docks, and parked at the top of the hill.

I looked out at the grey, swirling Irish Sea, the waves frothing up against the long thin piers, the knots of fishermen who seemed never to catch anything, standing on the ends.

I could see a large ship, a smudge of grey on the horizon, waiting a long way out. It would be holding chemicals for the Marchon plant. Small boats went in and out between the bigger ship and the docks, to load and unload mysterious substances. On the dockside was an enormous hopper attached to a chute that took what looked like roughly ground powder into the boats or out of the boats, I never knew which.

At Donnan's Quay a boat was in and men in donkey jackets and high visibility vests were unloading boxes of wriggling silver fish.

A shadow of clouds moved slowly across the grass, and the sky changed colour. It was as if a violet-tinged greyness was seeping up into it from out of the sea. Three o'clock and it was already growing dark.

I went to Carlisle but I can't remember going there or being there. I sat and looked at the baby through the glass but all I could think about was Fiona. The nurses helped me to feed her, a tiny centimetre of milk from a syringe each time. The milk had been expressed by someone else and came from a milk bank. I went every day and two weeks passed and I couldn't remember anything of what happened. I do remember I bought a soft toy, a pink hippopotamus, from the hospital shop and hung it on the end of her incubator. There was a concrete hippopotamus in Walsall town centre and Fiona and I used to joke about it and wonder what it meant.

In Birmingham we had a meeting with an undertaker who spoke quietly and nodded all the time.

He asked about floral tributes and Fiona's mother told him about Fiona's favourite flowers, and he said that they would be fine, but added that those particular blooms required attention with a hairdryer before the service in order to open up the petals properly.

He asked about psalms and gospels and offertories and all kinds of other things that I didn't understand. Then he asked us whether we wanted her body to lie in a chapel of rest for a few hours so people could go and see her; if so, we would need to think about what she might wear. Was there anything she would have preferred?

Fiona's mother took out a tissue and dabbed her eyes. 'I don't know, I don't know. She was twenty-five.'

'There's a band T-shirt,' I said. 'She loved it. I mean it was the one she wore the most.'

'Which one was it?' said the undertaker.

'The Jesus and Mary Chain.'

The undertaker looked at Fiona's mother for a sign of

agreement to this garment, but she was now crying and Melvin was holding her hand. His face looked clenched-up.

'She had some favourite shoes,' I said.

'She won't need shoes, don't worry,' the undertaker said,

Fiona's mother let out a loud cry. 'But why? Why not? Why not shoes? She was twenty-five.'

'Yes, Mrs Sumner, I know, I know, it's so hard,' the undertaker said. 'Of course. You can have whatever you like.'

The undertaker looked down at his list of questions. 'Now, what about make-up?' he said, using a soft voice which was barely audible. 'With someone so young we sometimes don't need to use any at all.'

'So that's a bonus,' said Fiona's dad.

At the funeral there were lots of people from her home town, from her old school, and from the university. There were even some fans of Pop Pop Pop!

Music was played, music her parents said she had liked when she was young. I thought that this music they played was too tuneful and I didn't like the way the priest called her Fiona-May all the time because, even though I knew she was called Fiona-May, no one called her that, not even her parents.

Someone read out a review they had written of one of her compositions. 'In her music, I hear a negotiation between human control and chance. Zig-zagging synth motifs rise out of the drones and return to them. At other points, she simply allows the instrument to play itself, leaving harmonics and timbral inconsistency to form shapes of their own accord. Long, sustained synthesiser notes falter gently, creating undulations in the texture like chips and dents on an antique. Drones curdle together to form overtones that flicker and dance above the central hums.' Everyone clapped and cheered at this.

I didn't know how to feel. Right down next to where you hurt the most is your medicine, a doctor in Cumbria had said to me. I thought about the things I liked about her. I liked the way she walked but I never told her that. I liked the shape of her feet but I never told her that either because I thought she'd think I was a weird foot fetishist. But I would look at them a lot when she was lying on the bed reading in her stockinged feet. I liked that she wore her shirts half un-tucked and half tucked, one way on either side, but I never told her that. I had never seen anyone else do that with their shirt and I never knew whether it was deliberate or just the way it fell as she walked about. I thought I should stand up and say all these things to the audience in the crematorium. But who was I? I had only known her for just over a year, so I felt as if I didn't know enough to stand up and say things in front of all these people. Someone asked me about her ashes. Did she have a favourite place? Maybe something to do with music? I didn't know. Maybe she would like her ashes to be crushed and impregnated into a piece of wood that could then be made into a violin, so that her molecules could endlessly vibrate with sound. But I don't know if she would have liked that sort of thing. Maybe if she had heard about that sort of thing she would have said oh my God, how *fake*, how *self-obsessed*.

The organist stabbed note clusters up and down the key-boards and held long deep pedal notes with his feet. Some avant-garde tune one of Fiona's friends had said she liked.

I wished she had been a superstitious Catholic like me. Even though I knew deep down that death was the end,

I held a parallel contradictory view that maybe there was another life and maybe people were looking down on us, walking among us, communicating with us, waiting for the time when we can all be together again. However much you learn about science and the universe, when you're a Catholic, this feeling never goes away. I thought about all the people in the world never dying, just looping round and round, endlessly dismantling and resolving themselves, and I thought that maybe I should stand up and say these things in the church.

But I couldn't.

I thought of what she had said that night when we were standing outside the Wheatsheaf. That when she was walking away from me she could feel herself shrinking on the surface of my eyeballs, becoming a little tiny dot. I thought about that as I sat in the church with everything else just washing over me.

The coach pulled into Carlisle coach station and I walked the mile or so out of the city centre to the hospital, where the baby was, where Katya was. It was late January, one of those freezing cold bright days without a breeze when you can't help but think about the future and you forget the darker days of winter stacked up behind you.

PART THREE

CHAPTER ONE

1989

The courtroom was full and every witness for the prosecution had been heard. Now it was the turn of the defence and I, as a key character witness, had been asked to take the stand and explain what had happened.

So I stood there in the court and told them everything.

It was interesting to watch the reactions of the people in the packed court room – the public in the gallery, the jury, the judge and the many solicitors and barristers. I knew that my account would help and that this might be the only way to save the situation.

I didn't go through every tiny detail, just the key sections, the sections that were vital to the case. But here I have included it all because I think it will help you to better understand what happened next.

As I spoke, members of the jury leaned forward in their seats, and solicitors took notes.

'Katya was one year and two months old in February 1989 when I took the phone call. I was living back in the West Midlands, in West Bromwich near Fiona's parents in a small 1930s semi I was renting. We had a nice set-up. People had gathered together and got us everything we needed to set up home for a new baby and a young father starting from nothing. Fiona's parents had found the house for me, and they liked it because it was so near to them. They could help with Katya. Their granddaughter. They loved Katya. They took her out to the nearby park every day and talked to her all the time telling her about everything they could see – the trees, the dogs, the plants, the playground, the animals in the urban farm. Katya had turned out to be a real fighter just as the doctor had said. She was still small for her age but when she came out of hospital – after nearly three months in the neonatal unit – she put on lots of weight very quickly. She did, however, look tiny compared to other babies of her age and everyone in the street used to stop us to have a closer look at her and say, my goodness, she looks like a little doll – isn't she lovely!

As far as work was concerned, I had given up my film journalism ideas for the time being and had found a voluntary job I really liked – helping other people with their problems down at the Citizens Advice Bureau. The manager said that for my age I brought a great maturity to the role and the clients liked me and often asked for me when they turned up in reception. Katya was beginning to talk. When she first said *Daddy* we were all excited but there was a poignancy there all the same – the fact that that she wouldn't ever really be able to say *Mummy* in the same way. That was hard, but that was something we all had to learn to stop thinking about. I would often be reminded, though. The health visitor, Mrs Keenan, would talk about her grown-up daughter all the time, about how the two of them were so close, and how they always did everything together – shopping, holidays, the gym, decorating. They had the same hairdresser. They could spend hours on the phone to each other – even after they had been together all day. Her own husband and her daughter's husband couldn't understand it. 'That's mothers and daughters,' Mrs Keenan would say, rolling her eyes.

I didn't think I would be able to replace that role for Katya. I hated shopping, for one thing. And also I had begun to worry about what would happen when I met someone else. There was the whole issue around another woman becoming a surrogate maternal figure, a stepmother, and I was of course familiar with the negative role stepmothers play in myth, popular culture and fairy stories. And I had noticed the role much more as I read classic stories to Katya. I sometimes edited out this aspect of the tales and made the character just an ordinary mother. But that made it worse: why would a real mother behave in that evil way?

That day, the day the phone call came, it was the middle of February, a Sunday. It was teatime, there was a mizzly grey sky, and darkness was falling. I had just taken Katya for a long walk around the shops in West Bromwich and then to the Sandwell Valley Country Park, and as the route home took me past their house, I had called in at Fiona's parents. The rocking motion of the pushchair had sent Katya to sleep, and she looked so comfortable and happy there I decided not to take her back outside right away into the damp and cold, as I knew this would wake her up. Instead I agreed to having some food at Fiona's parents, which was sandwiches of roast chicken left over from the dinner they'd had earlier that day, and we watched *Antiques Roadshow* together. I found it comforting to be there. Although Fiona was gone and this was tough for everyone, keeping up a strong relationship with Fiona's parents was in some way like maintaining my love for Fiona. Even including watching *Antiques Roadshow* and talking about the state of the housing market with Fiona's dad and about gardening with Fiona's mum.

'This current rate of interest can't be allowed to continue,' I remember Melvin was saying. 'One of my clients took out a mortgage the other day at $13\frac{1}{2}$ per cent. And they took it on a deferred interest-only deal which is going to come back and bite them badly. Negative equity is wiping people out in London and I think it will sweep its way up here too.'

'Yes,' I said.

'This winter's been way too mild,' her mother was saying. 'The shrubs are coming into bud too early and that's going to send everything out of kilter.'

'Yes,' I said.

I found it hard to visualise the two of them when they were young: she the high-kicking dancer with feathers on her head and a sparkly leotard, and he splashing the cymbals and brushing the snare behind her. And the brave rescue from the holiday camp fire – Mr Sumner breaking down a door and carrying her to safety through fume-filled corridors – and I wondered whether he believed he could have somehow saved Fiona in a similarly heroic and fearless way if only he'd been given the chance.

Now, it seemed safer to talk about things that had no direct relevance to us or to Fiona and in this way we always kept talking, filling the silence with noise. This was something all three of us were desperate to do. Now and again though, if there was a particularly long silence, Fiona's mum would mention it. Usually in relation to something I was supposed to have done. This time it was whether I had looked into taking legal action for medical negligence against someone in the health service.

'I'm not sure those Cumbrian doctors did everything right,' she kept saying. 'I found a book in the library about it, about pre-eclampsia, and it said that a pre-eclamptic fit was a medieval thing that only happened nowadays in Third World countries. No woman in a developed country should ever have been allowed to get to that stage. I'm not sure those Cumbrian doctors knew what they were doing.'

A woman on *Antiques Roadshow* was showing a gem-encrusted cruet set to a man in a tweed suit and they were at the valuation stage, which was the only point of interest in the programme.

I told Fiona's mother that I agreed the NHS hadn't been perfect and that I would look into it.

Her dad, Melvin, sighed and threw his head back against the back of the armchair. 'It's not going to bring her back though, is it? Legal advice. Compensation.'

'I didn't say it would bring her back,' Fiona's mother snapped.

'I didn't say you said it would bring her back,' he said slowly as if repeating an instruction for the hundredth time to a small child who never listened. 'Listen to the words I'm saying and the context of them and think about the phrases I am replying to.'

We stared at *Antiques Roadshow* and said nothing for a long time. A lady had brought along a display case of stuffed weasels which been posed as a jazz band. Normally we would have laughed at this archaic throwback, but today we didn't. As the camera nosed in close to a weasel playing a trumpet, the atmosphere of the room and the deadness of the silence seemed to emphasise the meaninglessness of this tableau, the pointlessness of eviscerating these poor animals, filling them with chemicals and sawdust, then posing them upright and attaching musical instruments to their paws to form this band of gruesome cadavers. To make things worse, the deathly puppet master had given a jaunty lurch to their shoulders, as if they had been frozen in mid musical phrase. This macabre diorama of death, this attempted reanimation of the spark of life, seemed to poison the air even more than that venomous exchange between Fiona's parents, and we shifted in our seats uncomfortably and waited long seconds until the dead weasel combo was gone from the screen.

Looking back at the timing of it all, it's almost as if the caller knew, as if she had been waiting for this precise mood to descend on our small family before she made the call, because she knew this mood would make me more willing to cooperate. She would catch me at a time when I felt desperate for something to change, to help me escape from this despondency, and it didn't really matter what that something was. Maybe I was wrong, maybe it was all just a series of unfortunate incidents.

But here's what happened.

The phone rang loudly and we jerked up in our seats as if we had been saved from something. Little Katya stirred in her pushchair, and made a whining sound.

Melvin went out to the hall where the phone sat on its little table and I heard him say, 'Yes, he is here, I'll fetch him.'

I had given everyone this number as there was no phone in my new place and I hadn't intended to get one.

'Hello,' I said, in a questioning, cautious tone.

The voice that came back was familiar.

It was Mathilde Pelletier.

'Quinn,' she said. 'I need to see you.'

'Mathilde? You're still in Birmingham?'

'Yes,' said Mathilde. 'And I need to see you. I've got myself into a little local difficulty and need your advice.'

Even though I knew that Mathilde Pelletier was just some fading actress from an obscure cult B-movie from the sixties there was something alluring and pleasantly disruptive about the idea of meeting her again. So I turned up at the allocated place – the large café above Rackhams department store on Caldmore Row – and there was Mathilde Pelletier dressed as usual in head-to-toe black and her long legs exposed as far as her upper thigh, her feet in three-inch heels.

But as soon as I got close I could see that she wasn't the calm and utterly-in-control vampish figure she had been the last time I saw her. Her face looked crumpled, as if it had been squeezed out of shape and had never sprung back, and there was a little electric twitch in a nerve at the corner of her mouth.

'My God,' I said, after we exchanged a kiss on the cheek, 'Mathilde, what's wrong? What's been happening to you?'

'Don't worry about me, Quinn. I'm a little stressed at the moment, that's all.' Her mascara had run, the dark pools against her pale make-up giving her the appearance of a vampire. She took out a red handkerchief with black poodles printed all over it, and dabbed her eyes.

'Get us some drinks, Quinn, and then you can tell me all about the baby and your domestic bliss in West Bromwich. I hear you are giving advice to those in far more need than me.'

Despite that initial show of interest, she enquired no further about my life from that moment on. As soon as I had poured out the tea, she began to tell me her story.

'It's this bloke I started seeing. It started out lighthearted but things quickly got a lot deeper. We became closely involved in a big way. Very, very intense.' She sniffed and took a long drink of her tea, then tapped a cigarette out of her packet of Gitanes and lit up. 'It was great for a short time, don't get me wrong. He smoked strong cigarettes and liked old films. We went for walks. We would go for miles. Drinking alcohol and caffeine. And cackling at things that weren't funny. And holding on tight to each other, like we were both drowning or something. But then, after a while, it turned out to be a big mistake. Now I just can't get rid of him. He won't take no for an answer, won't accept that we are finished. That it's over. I heard a noise outside my flat one night last week and when I looked out there he was, parked on the street, just staring up at my window. And when he saw me looking down at him, he didn't even wave, or move or flinch. Just continued to stare. I felt as though he had sent out a long tentacle that had crept inside me and was squeezing my soul till it hurt. I went back to bed. I'm a strong woman. I've lived on my own for many years, so I feel I can cope with this sort of thing. But nevertheless, I took a couple of pills to help me sleep. When I got up the next day he was still there, staring up at my window. He didn't come out of the car and knock on the door. He just sat there looking up.'

'How long have you known this man?' I asked her.

'We had a few dates and I'll admit that at first I liked his moodiness, his desperateness. He seemed like some kind of an outlaw and sometimes that's what you want. Battersby, the man is called. He is unpredictable and unafraid of doing things that are out of the ordinary. Like the first time I kissed him, he ran out into a busy dual carriageway, the Anson Road, took off his shoes, and threw them up in the air, juggling with them. All the traffic had to stop – can you

218

believe it? He said he did it because he was just so happy, that's what he wanted to do. I saw him a few more times but after a while he became weird. Very, very dark. Began to talk about death, about dying. He began to say that there was no future for him. And then he began to say that there was no future for me either. It was then that he said that we should make a suicide pact.'

At this point in my statement to the court you could hear members of the jury gasp softly, and there were a few intakes of breath.

'What?' I said putting my cup down hard on the table, making everyone in the café look over.

'Yes. A suicide pact. He said that we should die together. That was the only way we could both be happy. He said he knew a good way, a' – she paused and took a long draw on her cigarette – 'p-p-painless way to do it.' She had begun to cry again and I leaned over and gripped her hand. 'Painless, Quinn. That's what he said. Like I was one puppy too many or something. All we needed to do was agree a date, he said. He would do everything else. So the next time he rang I told him that it was all over. But he wouldn't accept it. "No it's not over," he kept saying. "It's in our destiny. It's in the stars. We are destined to be together for ever. We have to go through with it."'

'Have you told the police?'

'That's the other thing.'

'What?'

'He *is* the police. Detective Inspector Battersby.'

I paused my telling of the story to the courtroom at this point and looked over to the row of policemen in the courtroom, and the eyes of the jury looked in that direction too. But there was no visible reaction from the officers present.

There was, however, a lot of shuffling and muttering from the public gallery.

'For Christ's sake, Mathilde. What have you got yourself into? How did you end up with a policeman?'

'He was one of the detectives investigating Betty – that time when a couple of her Thursday jaunts went wrong.'

'Thursday jaunts? I only remember the time she got stuck in Dudley Zoo and the time she went to Sheffield and slept at the top of the crane.'

'Every Thursday she went off somewhere and no one knows where, or why. Or for who.'

'Betty's poor mother must have been out of her mind.'

'Well, she was rarely inside of it, so who would know the difference?'

'What do you mean?'

'Did you ever meet Betty's mother?'

'No.'

'Of course you didn't. No one ever did.'

'She was disabled, wasn't she? Housebound, according to Betty.'

'There was nothing wrong with her that wasn't self-inflicted. The bottle and the needle and the pipe were her signs of the cross. She didn't even notice when those Thursday jaunts went wrong. It was the neighbours who raised the alarm.'

'An addict – well, so what? She still needs Betty's support. Who do you think supplied her?'

'I don't know – Battersby himself maybe? That's the twisted world we live in. Don't worry about me, Quinn. It will all be OK. I'm just feeling a bit down with it all. I'm sure all will be fine.'

'Is there anything I can do? Quinn might sound like the name of a tough guy, but tough guy I am not.'

'You won't be able to do anything to help. I don't expect you to try. I just wanted you to listen to me. Battersby is not someone you can reason with. He is involved in all kinds of things. The Birmingham underworld. Doormen, drug dealers, nightclubs. That's what the police are like around here. They are not like normal people, like us. They are more like the gangsters. In fact they are worse than the gangsters. It's as if they have to be worse than them if they are to beat them. You see, Quinn, I've worked it out, I've been thinking about it. Policemen have the same desires, the same needs as the gangsters. But they have something extra. They have the means, and also they have the power. If you got involved, I really don't know what he would do to you. He could do anything. Make you disappear. I don't know. And he lives right there in the thick of it all, in the middle of this gang-run estate.'

I had run out of suggestions, run out of things to say. I just sat there gripping her hand watching her contort herself into a tangle of pain and worry, and I was unable to do anything to stop it happening. I looked beyond her, out of the window. The café was on the top floor of the store, giving a panoramic view of the city – the cathedral, the Rotunda, New Street Station. A light rain was beginning to fall, it was getting dark, and the roads were thickening with rush-hour traffic.

CHAPTER TWO

1989

Every night I made up stories for Katya to help her get to sleep. I knew she was too young to understand the fabulous tales of wonder I wove for her, but she would watch my mouth intently and seemed to like the rising and falling of my voice as I varied the tone and pitch and volume and did the funny voices for the talking animals and the various anthropomorphised inanimate objects. My favourite was a story about a talking fish called Henry who kept getting caught up in storms and ended up blown into trees in the park from where he would cry for help and me and Katya would climb up and get him down and drive him to the seaside where he lived with other sea creatures, all of which had their own names and voices and sometimes their own spin-off adventures as well.

That night I carried on telling Katya stories long after she had fallen to sleep. I think that I was telling them to myself to soothe my nerves. Later, in bed, I couldn't get to sleep. I lay for a long time thinking about Mathilde and the worrying Detective Inspector Battersby. I tried to clear my mind by telling myself some of the stories about talking animals that

I would tell to Katya. But my mind kept getting snagged up on the image of the stuffed weasels on *Antiques Roadshow*. Was that what I was doing with these stories? A sick form of imaginary taxidermy? And related to this I couldn't help thinking about the way Melvin had snapped so venomously at his wife. Something like this happening to a family could tear everything apart. Melvin and Barbara, Mathilde and Battersby, the stuffed animals, Katya's stories, everything spun around in my head as if all my problems had been stuck together and made into a gruesome carousel that I couldn't get off.

Sleep was beginning to creep in when I heard the pounding on the front door. My digital bedside clock said 4.30 a.m. I ran to the window and looked out and even through the rain and dark I recognised the shape of the person looking up at my window.

When Mathilde got inside she produced a bottle of whisky from her coat pocket and plonked it on to the kitchen table. I found two glasses and poured us both a big one. She slurped hers down like it was cool water and she'd been crawling through a desert for days. She did this three times before she would say anything, and I matched her drink for drink, because, to be honest, I felt I needed it too. After she had calmed down enough, she told me what had happened.

'It's Battersby,' she said.

'Yes?'

'Something has happened to him. I found out this evening, not long after I had seen you.'

She took a ripped-out newspaper page from her pocket and slid it across the table towards me.

The headline said POLICE INSPECTOR SUFFERS SHOTGUN WOUNDS.

Last night Detective Inspector Battersby of south Birmingham disturbed an armed intruder in his house and after a struggle, a shotgun went off. DI Battersby is recovering in hospital from serious wounding to his eyes. A hospital spokesman says that the inspector is comfortable but will need careful attention if his sight is to be saved. The intruder has not yet been found.

While I was reading the newspaper report, Mathilde took out a packet of Gitanes, tapped one out for herself, and offered me one too. I didn't normally smoke but I took it and I smoked non-stop for the next couple of hours. After I'd read the news item about Battersby my first thought was, it sounds like he had it coming, looks like he got what he deserved. But the more I thought about it as I sat there smoking and drinking whisky and looking at Mathilde who wasn't saying anything else, I wondered what else it could mean and what murky business I, Daniel Quinn, was being dragged into. I should have put an end to it there and then. I should have said, Mathilde, this has nothing to do with me, and I can't help you. You must sort this thing out for yourself. But I didn't do that, as you know. I smoked more cigarettes and drank more whisky. If I am honest, this drama, this heightened experience, was making me feel more alive than I had felt in months. And perhaps because Mathilde looked at me with such imploringly helpless eyes, and seemed to have faith in my abilities to tackle the problem of Battersby in some way, I really believed that I could do something to help her. I didn't know what, but I truly believed that if anyone was going to get her out of this mess then it would have to be me.

'At least he won't be sitting outside your house for a while,' I said.

'The problem is,' she said, 'I don't want the police to find out that I was connected to him.'

'How could that happen?'

'Oh, Quinn, I don't know,' she said, 'I'm just a nervous wreck about the whole thing,' and then she folded the newspaper page in half, and then in half again and went on folding until she could not make it any smaller, her hands trembling as she did so. 'I suppose I just always think the worst.'

'We will think of something,' I said, gripping her upper arm tightly. But in the time we sat there nothing occurred to either of us. So we just sat on the sofa drinking whisky and smoking for another hour. We tried to talk about other things, other subjects. I told her how great Katya was. I told her about the advice centre and how I helped people on welfare benefits with their money problems. Neither of us mentioned *Out of the Dark*, but that was a good thing because my feelings towards the film had become a little colder since what had happened to Fiona. Between whiskies I popped upstairs every now and again to check on Katya and each time I looked in she was spark out.

We drank the whole bottle of whisky and smoked two packets of Gitanes and then Mathilde suddenly seemed very tired, and she kicked off her high heels and pulled her feet up on to the sofa, and rested her head on my shoulder. She fell asleep quickly and her snoring was like the sound of a kitten purring. I didn't move from that position because I didn't want to disturb her. She was sleeping like someone who hadn't slept for days, as if a huge weight of worry had lifted from her and floated off into the sky.

Eventually I must have fallen asleep in that position, sitting up, because the next thing I knew a woman's sharp voice was saying, 'Mr Quinn, Mr Quinn,' and I woke with a start to see the health visitor Mrs Keenan standing over us. I remembered then that I had made an appointment for her to call round.

I stood up immediately and Mathilde flopped flat on to the sofa and, without opening her eyes, tried to continue her sleep. Her shoes were off and her skirt had ridden up, there was ash all over her front from the cigarettes, and her tights were laddered. The coffee table was covered in cigarette butts, many of which had missed the ashtray. The ripped-out newspaper page was lying there too, folded into a small square. The whisky bottle lay empty on the carpet, next to one of the glasses we'd been drinking from. The other glass looked as though it had been tossed against the tiled fire grate, because it was smashed into several pieces. I really didn't know how anything had ended up how it was.

To make matters worse I could hear Katya crying loudly upstairs, the sort of crying which is interspersed with massive gulps of air in between. I had no idea how long she had been awake.

'The front door was wide open,' Mrs Keenan said, 'anyone could have walked in off the street,' pointedly looking at Mathilde when she said this. 'Go to your daughter, Mr Quinn. It sounds as though she needs you.'

I ran upstairs and picked Katya out of her cot and cradled her to my chest. Her crying subsided to a whimper. I heard the front door slam and I saw Mathilde through the window, scurrying down the street, her feet wobbling on the high heels she'd just put back on.

Mrs Keenan had picked up most of the debris and carried it into the kitchen.

'I've wrapped the broken glass in newspaper and dropped it into the bin,' she said. 'You'll have to hoover though, in case there are any small bits.'

She was sitting at the kitchen table, her big A4 notebook open before her, and a pen poised.

'Do you have a Hoover, Mr Quinn?'

'Yes. Listen, I can explain, I'm —'

'Now,' she said. 'Can you tell me for the record who that woman is and what her relationship is with you and your daughter Katya?'

I couldn't think of anything to say.

'We have to look after the safety of that young child. Her well-being is uppermost in our minds and anything that might persuade us that being looked after here in this rented house by a lone twenty-five-year-old father might not be in her best interests means that we would have to re-examine the situation with great care and seriousness.'

'Twenty-six,' I said. 'I'm twenty-six now.'

'Is she a long-term friend? A girlfriend even?'

'No,' I said.

'Do you pay her?'

'What?' I said. 'No. Of course not. She is an ex-film star, if you must know.'

Mrs Keenan looked unimpressed. 'The baby's welfare comes first, Mr Quinn. That is our chief concern.'

It was two weeks later when I heard from Mathilde again. I had vowed for my sake and Katya's sake that I would never have her in my home again. Although Mrs Keenan had read me the riot act, luckily she had not escalated the matter further. As far as I knew.

I was at Fiona's parents' house helping Katya build a tower of bricks on the mat when the phone went and something in its insistent repetition, a ding ding ding ding that just wouldn't give up, told me who it was.

I have always wondered what entitles some people to say only the words *it's me*, and then pause for a long time. Fiona used to be the only *it's me* person and I didn't think Mathilde had really earned an *it's me* introduction.

After the long pause, she went on. 'He's been discharged. Battersby's been discharged.' She was breathless, and spoke rapidly. 'According to the newspapers he is back home. His eyes are bandaged and he needs to rest and stay inside, out of the light, to allow the eyes to heal. But I'm worried the police might find something in his flat that links him to me.'

'What would that be?'

'He has a suicide note we wrote together. Signed by us both.'

At this point in my statement I stopped. A dramatic pause, you could say. I wanted to make sure that the key points of information sank in. Voices were raised in the courtroom but it wasn't clear what they were saying.

'Oh, Quinn,' said Mathilde, 'I don't know what I'm going to do.'

I'm not sure why, but it was at this point that I decided I would help her. Because it seemed to me that if you can't help someone in that situation – a woman terrorised by a corrupt man in a position of power – a dangerous man, an unpredictable man – then what was I on this earth for? I looked at Katya sitting on the floor building her tower of blocks and I thought about Fiona. Then I thought about all the women in the world and how society treated them and I didn't want Katya growing up in a world where men conspired to hide the evil actions of other men while men like me, the liberal, lefty men, stood by and did nothing about it, other than write articles for publications like the *Guardian*, and talk righteously down the pub.

'I'll go and see him,' I said. 'Just give me his address. I won't say who I am. I'll invent a reason and just turn up there and maybe I'll see that note and be able to retrieve it for you – who knows? It will help that his eyes are bandaged.'

She told me about the sideboard where he kept all his papers and letters and where the suicide note would be and what it looked like. She told me his address. She told me that there would be a nurse there looking after him, and probably a police guard.

Standing there in that courtroom reading out this account, I began to imagine the whole episode as a film, and I could see in my head all of the scenes being played out in a dark cinema to a hushed audience on the edges of their seats.

The next scene begins with a crane shot of me with Katya in her pushchair walking down an elegant curved street of semis in the suburbs. Blossom trees everywhere. Shiny family cars, all exactly the same shape and colour, are parked in every drive. Men who look oddly alike are clipping hedges, women, also strangely alike, are outside doing things with flowers in the decorative borders. For this part of the story, if you don't mind, I will refer to myself in the third person. Quinn, just Quinn. On the soundtrack we hear Quinn's footsteps loudly, too loudly, and this effect will continue through this last sequence of scenes, growing even louder in the closing sections as if the slap slap of the heels on these hard city surfaces is the sound of a pursuing nemesis.

Under the sound of his footsteps we hear soft music growing louder. Strings, sweet-sounding at first, but slowly becoming discordant.

Quinn stops at a house and Fiona's mother opens the door and kneels before Katya, laughing and making funny noises, which we can't hear because of the now much louder strings on the soundtrack.

Cut to Quinn on the top deck of a double-decker bus, looking worried.

A cello joins the high-pitched violins, crawling down a long, slow atonal scale so it becomes a grumbling, purring noise beneath a chord of two high notes only a semitone apart which keeps moving up and down the scale. It is a soundtrack we recognise as the stuff of horror or suspense films.

Quinn takes out a scrap of paper with the address on it. He looks at it, then out of the window at a parade of tatty, shuttered-up shops where you could get home-brewing kits, second-hand fridges, house clearances, and quick loans with no questions asked.

A small child in the seat in front of Quinn waves a plastic doll at him but he looks at the child and doll and doesn't even smile. It's as if he isn't really there. This is no longer the Quinn we knew. It's as if he is a somnambulist, as if he has numbed himself so he can do this difficult task without thinking, as if he has removed himself from reality for a time.

He takes out an A-Z of Birmingham, looks at it quizzically with the scrap of paper next to it, then leans forward towards the mother of the child.

'Any idea where I would get off the bus for this place?' he says, showing her the address.

'Blimey,' she says. 'Someone like you doesn't want to be going there. It's the Wild West.'

'I'll be OK,' he says, sitting back in his seat.

Through the window of the bus he sees a big poster.

A new vision for Birmingham – the regeneration of the Bull Ring and the Rotunda – have your say in the public consultation at Birmingham Voluntary Service Council, Digbeth

Cut to him getting off the bus and we see him from high up, a tiny marooned figure on a long empty road with nothing on it but the edges of rundown-looking estates. The camera cuts to the back of the bus turning the corner and then cuts back to Quinn. Still not another soul around. He begins to walk. A car roars past and sounds its horn as if at Quinn. We see from his point of view a long straight road disappearing into the distance with no people, buildings or vehicles on it, like a technical line drawing. Cut to Quinn walking towards the camera with the same long featureless road behind him.

A sign says Shakespeare Boulevard.

He looks down at his A-Z and then turns down a side road.

He passes a tin-shed one-pump petrol garage with a sign saying *pay before you pump*.

He passes a scrap-metal yard.

He passes a ramshackle building that says *Little Glen's Boxing Club*. Silhouettes of boxers training in the windows.

He passes a flat-roofed pub called the Lemon Tree.

Then the entrance to a council estate looms up in front of him.

A large sign says *Lichfield Park* with a list of the streets, closes, crescents, walks, ringways and avenues under it.

Groups of lads on bikes are hanging about everywhere.

A couple of them shout over to him but he ignores them. He turns down a street that leads to another street and then he turns down that one. The route he is taking makes it feel as though he is entering a labyrinth. Each street gets narrower and narrower and just as we think it's a cul-de-sac, another small walkway leads him to yet another street and he keeps going like this, deeper and deeper into the centre, glancing at his A-Z all the time. The sky has turned a soft dusky dark and the streets are lines of hazy lights with the darting silhouettes of figures moving in and out of them. He looks at his watch. 4.30 p.m. Dark winter days. We realise that since he has entered the housing estate the soundtrack has become quieter, and all we hear now is the clump clump clump of Quinn's feet on the tarmac.

Eventually, Quinn comes to a stop outside a particular house, which looks very dark as if there is no one in it. Two uniformed policemen are standing outside the front door, one either side. Then the camera pulls away again and we see from a distance Quinn walking up the path towards the policemen.

'What are you after, mate?' one of them says.

'I'm doing a survey for the council,' Quinn says.

The policemen laugh and shake their heads.

'Not the best of times, but if you must,' says one.

Quinn knocks on the door.

Nothing happens.

He knocks again and the camera pulls back to show a curtain moving, and then a woman in a nurse's uniform opens the door.

'I'm looking for Mr Battersby,' says Quinn.

She looks at the policemen and they shrug.

'You're not from the papers, are you?' she says.

'I'm running a consultation for the city council. It's about the redevelopment of the Bull Ring. Pulling down the Rotunda and all that. You will have seen it in the papers.'

A voice calls out, 'Let him in.'

The nurse ushers him down the hall. 'Mr Battersby is unwell. He has had an operation on his eyes, poor man, and he needs to rest while his sight recovers. Just remember he can't see anything and he's not supposed to move about.'

Cut to Battersby's front room. It is sparsely furnished with a dining table, a couple of chairs in the centre, and a sideboard with a drawer. The drawer that Mathilde told Quinn about.

There is a photo of a boxer on the wall and in the corner a huge glass case with a full-sized stuffed wolf in it, like you'd see in a museum. Quinn would be thinking about the stuffed weasels when he sees this. But this is no Victorian comedic tableau.

There are no lights on inside the house, but the orange-tinged glow from the street lamp outside shows Battersby sitting at the table. He has a bandage across his eyes but appears to be looking in the direction of Quinn. There is a pillow on the table to rest his head on while his eyes heal. Battersby's head is completely bald, there are pock marks all over his face from the shotgun pellets, and he has a neatly trimmed beard and moustache in van Dyck style. A dark-coloured tattoo plunges from his neck down under his white T-shirt, which is tightly fitted and shows a muscly, worked-out physique, further emphasised by the swift, purposeful way he moves his upper body. The bandage across his eyes is stained brown and yellow at the sides.

Quinn hasn't seen this cop before. The man is definitely not, despite what Mathilde said, one of the policemen who helped with the hunt for Betty. This policeman looks like an altogether different kind of cop, the sort of cop who is attracted to the dark side of the job, who likes the dirtiness of crime, who likes to live in the same dirt as the criminals, to touch the dirt and taste the dirt, especially the dirt in secret places that light never reaches.

A radio is playing, a noisy phone-in, people shouting

about football. *The problem with the Villa is this, the problem with the Villa is that.*

'Mr Battersby?' the nurse says. 'I'll leave you with this young man for a few moments while I go and see another patient.'

'Fine, fine,' he says.

Quinn looks at the stuffed wolf. It is poised as if the animal has just heard or smelt something, its head cocked to the side and its tongue hanging out. Its coat is a murky grey colour with patches of dirty yellow – almost the same colours as Battersby's eye bandage.

'That's Sadie,' Battersby says. 'Sexy Sadie.'

Quinn looks about the room.

'The wolf. She's called Sexy Sadie. I guess that's what you were looking at. Everybody is fascinated by her. When I first got her there were loads of questions. Where did you find her, where did she used to live, how was she killed, all that. Well, all I know is that she's mine now and she's not going anywhere.'

'I'm going door to door with a council consultation,' says Quinn.

Battersby tilts his head this way and that as Quinn speaks, as if listening attentively to distant music.

'It's about the plan to knock down the Rotunda. There's a model on display at the Voluntary Service Council in Digbeth and we want people to have a look at the model and then tell the council what they think.'

'I don't like the Rotunda. I like old buildings. Stone buildings.'

'You might agree with these plans then. When do you expect your eyes to be better? I'll come round and show you the pictures.'

There is a long silence during which Battersby rests his head on the pillow.

'That nurse,' he says, from his position on the pillow. 'What's she look like?'

'I don't know.'

'Good-looking?'

'I suppose.'

'She brushes against me when she changes my dressing, and it's a bit intimate. But I don't know what she looks like. It could be some ancient old crone that I'm lusting after.'

'She looks OK to me,' says Quinn.

'Your type?'

Quinn laughs awkwardly. 'I don't know.'

'Does she have a nurse's uniform on?'

'Yes.'

'Silver lining. Ask me about the Bull Ring, then. Get on with your job.'

'Do you walk about in the city centre much?'

'To be honest, I mostly drive. Birmingham is made for cars. Good for moving but bad for stopping, that's what they always say about Birmingham.'

As Battersby speaks, Quinn moves over to the sideboard and puts his hand on the handle of the drawer. He looks over at Battersby whose head is still on the pillow.

A caller on the radio says that taking the ball off the Villa is like taking sweets off a baby.

'I almost never go into the centre now. They've made a right balls-up of it. The high street, for example, used to be an ancient right of way because there was a slaughter-house at the end. People had to be allowed to drive their beasts through it. That's why they leave the Palisades open all night. Because it's a legal thoroughfare.'

Quinn tugs hard on the drawer handle but it is stuck.

Another caller on the radio is saying the problem with the Villa is the chronic lack of investment in players.

'In the old days,' Battersby says, 'you could get from Snow Hill Station to the Bull Ring without crossing a road, it was all underpasses. There used to be a gentle slope from St Martin's Church all the way up. They should have kept that gentle slope. You still there?'

Quinn takes his hand away from the drawer.

'Yes.'

Battersby lifts his head form the pillow and points it in Quinn's direction.

'You've moved.'

'I was looking at the photo on your wall. The boxer.'

The photo is a framed black and white eight by ten of a skinny man in baggy white shorts, crouching below the camera, his gloved fists up and an angry taunting look on his face, like he was about to throw a jab at the photographer.

'Did he win a lot of fights?'

'West Midlands featherweight champion 1973. A great fighter and a great drinker and a great man for the ladies too. But a terrible father. Never saw hide nor hair of him until I had my first job in the police and then he came crawling.'

Quinn tugs at the drawer again and this time he manages to pull it out a little, but it won't come out any further. He looks over at Battersby.

'Boxing was his way out, and it worked for a short time. But he forgot to take anyone with him. Such as his family.'

Quinn puts two hands on the drawer and tugs as hard as he can and the drawer suddenly slides all the way out and tips up, sending everything clattering on to the wooden floor, and Quinn drops the drawer on top of it all.

'Shit,' Quinn says. 'Sorry.'

Letters, envelopes, paperclips, packets of pills, pens, all kinds of stuff, lie in heaps.

Battersby stands up. 'Hey, what's going on, man? Be careful over there.'

The camera cuts to the mound of debris from the drawer and then tracks along it until it comes to a purple envelope with *To The West Midlands Police* written on it. It is stamped and ready to post.

'Sorry. Looking for a pen.'

Battersby stands up, and with surprising speed for a man who was temporarily blind, crosses the room and stands right in front of Quinn.

'Give me your hand,' he says.

Quinn holds out his hand and Battersby grabs it. A close-up shows Battersby's enormous hand wrapped around Quinn's small fist. Battersby squeezes and Quinn grimaces. Cut to Battersby's face, his mouth slightly open and his brow furrowed as he concentrates on inflicting pain.

'Are you ready for the sacrament?'

'What?'

Battersby keeps squeezing, his cheeks and lips quivering with the effort, his face reddening. 'The sacrament. Do you feel you are ready?'

The squeezing gets harder. A caller on the radio says that the Villa are like school kids running in a line after the ball.

'Please,' Quinn says. 'I don't know.'

Battersby drops Quinn's hand.

'Because I think I am ready and when you think you are ready that's when you are. Want me to tell you about the town centre? I think that every town centre should have a graveyard. Because you can walk about in it and feel the

237

dead bodies under your feet. So it makes you think about what's really important. It gives you perspective. Do you ever think like that?'

'I like graveyards, yes.'

'It's a funny thing to say, but I sometimes go to grave-yards and stand by the graves, and I think about the dead bodies lying down there, all peaceful, and I think about the people around here, on this estate, struggling to live on a flea's fart of nothing, with the electric and the gas threaten-ing to cut them off, the car failing its MOT, the kids needing school uniforms, the loan men hammering down the doors, and I think – where is the better place to be? If you're hon-est? I get myself into a state of mind so that I find myself envying the dead. I've been thinking now that it might have been better if he'd finished me off.'

He says nothing for a time. The camera pulls back to show a two shot of them standing facing each other in si-lence, the stuffed wolf and the photo of the boxer also in shot.

'I wake up crying in the night,' Battsersby says, quietly. 'Have done for months. I used to lie there and stare into the darkness and I would see shapes, menacing shapes that seemed to be plotting against me. Then I would put the light on and they would disappear. But now with this' – he taps the bandage – 'there's no escape from the dark and the shapes that live there. What do you think of Sexy Sadie?'

'The wolf? I like it.'

'I thought about getting a dog. A real dog, a live dog. But whenever I find something I like, I always want to own it completely, to control it, and make it everlasting. And the only way I can think of doing that is by stopping it from changing. Permanently. That way I can keep it in the same state for ever. Keep it for me. Keep it perfect. Change frightens me. You find something or someone you love, be it a dog, a good friend, or a woman, and you want to keep it as it is, for ever, in the same state, don't you? We all do. You got a girlfriend?'

'She died,' Quinn says.

'Oh. God. So sorry, and me going on about graveyards. I had no idea.'

He goes over to his chair, bumping into the corners of the table as he moves, and then sits down again and rests his head on the pillow.

'I'll tell you what I think about the city centre. The whole city centre, in my humble opinion, is a mess and always will be. They've sent everything underneath. And because of this you will see that right in the middle of town, there's a hump. Have you noticed it? The hump is for the double-decker buses. To get their big backs through. Because they have to go underneath. Everything does.'

He begins to speak slowly, as if in a dream.

'They should have just sent the buses round the back but they had to send them underneath. That's why they have that hump.'

While he is speaking Quinn leans over and reaches down to the floor for the purple envelope.

'They should have kept that slope,' Battersby says. 'That gentle slope I told you about? They should have made the buses go round the back.'

Then we hear the clunk of the front door and the nurse's voice. 'Everything all right, Mr Battersby?'

A caller on the radio says that the Villa have the whole of their future before them.

CHAPTER THREE

1989

Quinn walks down the road away from the house. It is completely dark and the camera follows him from behind as he winds his way through the complicated housing estate. He keeps getting into cul-de-sacs and having to go back on himself. Again his footsteps sound very loud in the mix – slap, slap, slap. At each change of direction there is a cut to a different set of boys on bikes watching him.

Quinn is beginning to seem completely lost. At every point where he thinks he knows the way out, he spots another set of boys on bikes down an alley blocking his way, and he changes direction only to find yet another set of boys forming a human barrier. The whole thing begins to resemble a hall of mirrors or some other trick of the eye.

Eventually he finds a newsagent's and goes inside. We see him through the window asking the shopkeeper directions. The man points and waves his arms about and Quinn nods.

Cut to inside the shop as Quinn is leaving and we see him looking at a sidebar on the front page of the local paper.

Injured policeman – intruder identified

The camera noses in on a grainy photo of the man.

The photo is of John Ireland.

At this point the music returns: long, low, unresolved piano chords, topped by staccato high-pitched out-of-tune note clusters which jar the ears.

Quinn picks up the paper and holds it closer. The blurry picture of John Ireland fills the screen. Unusually for him, John Ireland is wearing a suit and tie and it looks as though he is on a stage at some sort of formal celebration with banners behind him.

If anyone has seen this man please do not approach him but call the police.

Quinn's face is expressionless, registering nothing. But the low chords and high dissonant stabbing notes on the soundtrack say it all.

Cut to a shot from inside the shop of Quinn's dark figure disappearing up the street.

Then a cut to him at the exit of the estate.

A brightly lit double-decker bus passes by, with no one on it.

Just as he is about to escape on to the main road the kids on bikes appear, blocking the way in front of him.

'You a child molester?' says one. They laugh.

'I was just with that copper who got shot,' Quinn says. 'Did you know you had a copper living on this estate?'

'Where you going now, student boy?'

'I want to get a bus back into town.'

'I want to get a bus back into town,' the kid repeats. 'Well, you've got to pay a toll to get past us,' he said. 'You have to give us your dinner money.'

They all laugh.

'I bet you lost a lot of dinner money when you were a kid.'

'I bet that's why you're such a fucking shrimp,' says another.

Quinn moves forward as if to push past them, then we hear a car pull up with a squeal of tyres and the boys scatter.

The door of the police car opens and a man in uniform jumps out and bundles Quinn into the back.

What follows is a silent trip through the suburbs into the centre of Birmingham. Piano music plays, a rambling series of unrelated out-of-tune chords which never resolve into anything familiar, and are each allowed to slowly decay to nothing before the next one comes in.

The lights of the city flash past.

Close-up on Quinn's hands, clenching and unclenching.

The Rotunda. The Bull Ring. We head through the centre and out the other side to the north-west. We see the policeman's view of the road ahead, the lit-up off-licences and huge produce shops of Handsworth, the vegetables and fruit piled high outside.

Close-up on Quinn's hands clenching and unclenching.

Takeaways and curry houses, barber shops, Asian dress shops, gold exchanges.

In West Bromwich the car pulls up outside a police station.

Quinn is sitting at a desk in an interview room, staring at the back of his hands which are laid out flat in front of him. Men's voices are shouting in the distance. A man is singing *and now the end is near* and another man shouts *shut the fuck up.*

Everything echoes. Faintly in the distance someone is whistling a tune, and it gets louder and closer and then the door opens and a policeman comes in, still whistling, adding frills and decorative adornments to the melody. He is carrying a big portable cassette player and he plants it roughly on the desk, then sits opposite Quinn.

He has a large bald head, a clean-shaven face, and a mouth which is very small, like a short slot between his flabby cheeks. He hardly seems to open this slot, even when he speaks, as if the words come from inside his throat.

'Just tying up some loose ends,' he says.

He puts down a pad and a pen, clicks on the tape recorder and tells it the date and time and who is in the room.

'Before you say it, yes, it was me on *Sale of the Century*. Garden furniture, a microwave, and a weekend for two in York, if you must know. Now, just for the level, tell me – what is your favourite type of snivelling little worm?'

'I like the red ones.'

The policeman looks at Quinn for a long time. 'The red ones.'

'Is that OK?'

'There's no right answer.'

'I mean is it OK for the level?'

'How long have you known John Ireland, Mr Quinn?'

'He called round one night and asked if he could rent my garage from me...'

Slow dissolve here to Quinn saying, '...then I had my own issues up home in Cumbria and I haven't seen John Ireland since.'

'You've seen his friend though?'

'Friend?'

'Agnes Mathilde Pelletier. Exotic French woman who looks as though she accidentally ran into somebody's fists at some time. Wasn't your fists, was it?'

At this point Quinn thinks it is best for him to lie to the police. With hindsight it would probably have been better to tell the truth but sometimes you have to lie to get the real truth across. Some things are truer than the truth, and this was one of those times.

'I haven't seen her since I got back from Cumbria,' Quinn says.

The policeman's large hairless head fills the screen, and his tiny slot of a mouth parts slightly as he speaks. 'She was in that old film, wasn't she? I couldn't make head nor tail of it.'

'I saw in the paper that John Ireland had been accused of shooting someone. I knew that was not in his nature and so I thought I would do a bit of private investigation. Stupid idea. But I liked him. *Like* him, I mean.'

'That's one way to look at it,' the policeman said. 'First thing we learn at police college is there's more than one way of looking at everything. How did you find out Battersby's address?'

'Rang a couple of Battersbys in the Birmingham phone book and said I had an important package for him.'

'You'd think they'd be more careful, wouldn't you? With what happened. Your phone record will check all this out of course, won't it?'

'All the calls were from phone boxes. But I suppose there'll be records at the other end.'

'What do you think is the second thing we learn at police college?'

'How to bake muffins?'

The big bald head didn't move and the little slot mouth didn't open.

'Sorry.'

'The second thing we learn is that truth is 80 per cent assumption and 20 per cent facts.'

'Did John Ireland have a motive to kill Battersby?'

'Who said John Ireland was trying to kill him?'

'Whoever the intruder was – because it might not have been John Ireland – fired a shotgun into Battersby's face, didn't he?'

'Did he?'

'That's what the papers say.'

'The papers say what we tell them to say.'

'Doesn't look like he went there to sell him cleaning products.'

'Papers said it was a disturbed robbery. So maybe we don't need a motive?'

'Maybe it *was* a robbery. And maybe it *wasn't* John Ireland.'

'Anyway, we will find a motive. We are going to search those famous garages everyone knows all about. Maybe we'll find something that links him to Battersby. Maybe Battersby is bent. You thought about that? Maybe Ireland owed him money. Maybe it was some deal gone sour. Maybe there was a double-cross. It will all come out in the end.'

'But why did you think it was him in the first place?'

'He drove there in a bright orange van with his name on the side.'

Quinn looked down at his hands again as if in the veins on the backs of them he would see an answer to this.

'You found him, then?' Quinn said finally.

'We thought *you* might know where he is.'

'I haven't kept in touch with him or Agnes Mathilde Pelletier.'

'It's Thursday tomorrow,' he says. 'It was always a Thursday when little Betty Fleming disappeared mysteriously and then came back. Does that mean anything to you? Being the same day? Things always happening on a Thursday?'

'Benefit day for her mother, I would expect.'

The policeman clicked off the machine. 'Just remember, Mr Quinn. This world. You are not part of this world. Don't get involved. You're out of your depth already and this is just the paddling pool.'

Cut to the Yew Tree Estate from high above. The two blocks of flats, the row of eight garages, featureless squares and oblongs of little Lego houses. The camera coils around the scene from above then spirals down past the flats and in front of the garages to the disused bus shelter at the side of the garages. An invisible typewriter punches the date in white text across the screen – Thursday 22 February. The word Thursday is in bold and bigger than the rest.

The camera glides inside the dilapidated bus shelter. Beer cans, broken bottles and cigarette butts litter the floor. We settle on a figure huddled up on the bench beside a cracked and grimy window. It is Quinn and from this hiding place he can see the garages. His head jerks up, he has been asleep, but something has roused him. He opens his eyes and we cut to little Betty in the small gap between the garages and the wall behind them. She is moving a section of corrugated iron that is leaning against the back of one of the garages. Her face looks older, with a more serious expression on it. A certain slowness, solemnity and deliberation to her move-ments gives her the appearance of a miniature middle-aged lady. She glances to the side, to check she is unobserved, then removes a panel from the back of one of the garag-es and places it on to the floor. Then she inserts the whole length of her arm inside this space and stands on her tiptoes to reach in. After some struggling, she pulls out a package which she stuffs into her rucksack.

The oldest trick in the book – the false back. All those garages would look empty to anyone looking in through the front door.

Package safely stowed, Betty hurries off and once she is out of sight Quinn darts out of the bus shelter and follows her at a safe distance. She gets on a 51 to Birmingham city centre and Quinn doesn't follow her further.

A tight close-up on Quinn's face.

'I knew,' Quinn says in voiceover, 'that when she got to Birmingham she'd head to Digbeth Coach Station or New Street Station, from where she could get out of town. It didn't matter where. It could be anywhere. What mattered was a pattern had formed, a cat's cradle of connections. When John Ireland's wife told me why he wanted all the garages, what she said had meant a lot to me. To keep those dark interiors bare, to keep them full of nothing, to own an empty space and preserve it that way. A noble and pure thing to desire. Like some sort of poetry. And now John Ireland's dream has been poisoned.'

CHAPTER FOUR

1989

Quinn dialled the number and it rang for a long time, eventually being picked up by an Ansamachine. The voice was unmistakable. That sleepy drawl, that distracted tone, as if she was doing something else at the same time as she spoke, such as painting her toenails.

We hear her distorted voice. 'This is Mathilde Pelletier. Pelletier. Yes. Like the fur people. The skinners. I am not here at the moment. Well I am, I am recording this' – small giggle – 'I cannot come to the phone because I am elsewhere. Doing something more important than talking to you, than waiting around for you to ring, which you never do. But I listen to these messages whenever I can and I will listen to yours with great interest. Please leave it after the machine goes *booooop*...'

Quinn pulled the phone away from his face and looked at the mouthpiece.

A jump-cut here to the tape curling around the wheels of the miniature cassette then a track back to show Mathilde lying on a bed smoking and staring at the Ansamachine.

Quinn's voice comes out of it. 'Mathilde, are you there?

Are you there? I've been to Battersby's. I've been interviewed by the police as well. You didn't tell me about John Ireland. Did you ask him to do that?'

Close-up on Mathilde's face as she listens to Quinn recording his message.

'Answer me, Mathilde. I know you are there, I know you are listening. John Ireland for Christ's sake, Mathilde. Mathilde, we saved him. And now this. When we first met you hadn't fallen down the stairs, had you? That was Battersby who did that to you, wasn't it? Was it something to do with Betty and her Thursday delivery trips?'

The camera is moving closer and closer into Mathilde's face as we hear Quinn speak, until all we see is a giant close-up of her eyes.

'There was a letter at Battersby's house like you said. The nurse will most likely have posted it by now.'

Mathilde reaches over and picks up the phone.

'Come to the grave that has no flowers,' she says. 'In three days' time.' And then she hangs up.

Cut to a long shot from outside, and the camera circles the phone box as if it is a predatory animal waiting for Quinn to come out. Finally he puts down the receiver and sags to his knees on the floor, a tiny figure screwed up on the floor like a bundle of rags.

What is he thinking? What is Quinn thinking? There, lying there, in the bitter cold on the piss-dirty floor of a battered-up phone box in the dark, alone. Is he the protagonist in this mini film noir, or is the protagonist John Ireland? If it is John Ireland, does that make Quinn just a side character, a mere bit part? That's the problem with real life compared to film. In films we know who the main characters are. It is their fortunes, their futures, their decisions that matter. But in real life we are all equal. All of our futures are important and all of our decisions matter. So how can we ever know what to care about? He was probably imagining himself as like Hamish from *Out of the Dark*, poor hapless Hamish, and wondering what Hamish would do. Hamish would, of course, do whatever Eva asked of him.

Cut to Quinn's view from the floor of the phone box. Cars and trucks going by. A post office van passes.

Outside the central sorting office Quinn stands in the street watching men unloading sacks of mail out of a truck. They have formed a short line and one man throws the bags out of the back of the vehicle, the next man passes them to the next, and the last man tosses them into the loading bay. Quinn watches these rhythmic actions – the swaying and dipping of the men's shoulders, the bags flying through the air, the constant movement down the line of men – and we see his head moving as he follows the motion; it seems to hypnotise him. A shot from above of Quinn watching the men loading the bags looks like a strange narrative painting, the sort of old picture that everyone used to understand, but was now nothing but a fascinating enigma.

Later everything seems darker, everything feels edgier.

Quinn walking down a long street of parked cars. He is wearing thick gloves and a hooded coat. He looks in the car windows and tries the doors of certain cars. He finds one open – a white Vauxhall Cavalier. He sits in it and looks about him nervously, then he takes out Mathilde's big screwdriver and jams it into the ignition and turns it. The engine fires up and we see him driving off.

We see the car exiting the city and we see him approaching the housing estate where Battersby lives.

He stops the car near a small playground on a hill high up above the estate. He can see Battersby's house. The police guard has gone.

The car radio plays 'Human' by Human League. Quinn watches the estate. He is smoking. His usually clean-shaven face is stubbly. His skin looks sweaty. He looks nothing like the man we have come to know.

We see lights going on and off in houses. We see silhouettes of the kids on their bikes. Close-up of several cigarettes in the car's ashtray showing he has been there a while. We see people leaving the boxing club. We see people leaving the Lemon Tree, the concrete flat-roofed pub we saw earlier. We hear shouting, and we keep cutting back to Quinn sitting in the car parked up high on the hill above the estate looking down on it all, smoking.

Cut to Quinn in his house at night.

The lights are off and he is looking out of the window. Every time a figure appears on the street he jumps back so he can't be seen.

Cut to a car in flames in a derelict yard. We recognise it as the Vauxhall Cavalier.

Cut to Katya asleep in her cot.

Quinn is stroking her head while reading a letter.

A close-up on the letter shows a header that says Sandwell MBC Child Protection. *Katya Quinn* in bold type in the middle. We cannot read the rest of the words.

The next morning, in the kitchen, he clicks on the radio, and the news comes on.

The police inspector from Birmingham who was recently shot and temporarily blinded has been found dead in his home. No further details are available on the cause of death or whether anyone else was involved.

Close-up on a coloured illustration of a tiger sitting at a

table drinking a cup of tea. Pull back to reveal the tiger is with a small girl and her mother. Pull back further to show Quinn reading the book to Katya.

Pull back yet further to show Quinn and Katya on a train cutting through the countryside.

The train pulls into Dover.

They board a ferry as foot passengers – tickets are checked, Quinn's passport is inspected.

Cut to Quinn holding Katya at the front of the ferry watching the prow cutting through the waves. Music rises up and Quinn smiles at Katya. She is holding the toy pink hippopotamus that had been hung on the end of her incubator.

The camera pans away to show Calais docks coming nearer.

We hear Quinn singing 'Frère Jacques' to Katya. The music on the soundtrack grows louder, a deep thudding bass like the engine of the ship. Then it darkens, thickens, and rises to a cacophonous arrhythmic carpet of noise, mixing with Quinn's singing. The camera closes in on the white frothing waves, then pans to the front of the boat. The bow doors are lowered on to the quay. Dark liquid gushes from a spout on the side of the boat, seagulls swoop low, shrieking, like the distant screams of children. The heady, disturbingly dissonant music and the screaming of the gulls gradually drown out the sound of Quinn singing.

Cut to a cemetery, then pan over to a plain-looking head-stone, a grey block that lies flat and says *Samuel Beckett 1906–1989*. A rectangular plastic pot of green and pinkish heather stands at its foot. No tributes have been left on the stone, there is nothing on it at all except for a few small pale yellow leaves that have fallen from the trees above. It looks like a barren concrete slab, a wall with only emptiness beyond.

A slim, gloved hand appears and places something on the grave. We don't see what it is.

Cut back to Quinn on the ferry with Katya. The camera pans over to another ferry in the dock which is being loaded up on its way back to Dover. A long line of cars with over-loaded roof-racks is moving slowly on to the vessel. We see Quinn watching this from the deck of the incoming ferry.

Then we see him pick up a newspaper and read it. Inside we see another report about the case.

Birmingham Police Shooting

A 47-year-old man from the West Bromwich area named John Ireland has been arrested and is helping the police with their enquiries in connection with the dead police inspector in Birmingham.

Cut to Quinn and Katya walking into the arrivals lounge at the ferry terminal in Calais. He stands holding Katya and looks over at the passport control desk without moving towards it. The stream of exiting passengers pushes past him, but he doesn't shift out of the way. A high shot shows him standing motionless like a stone in a river as the crowd makes its way around them.

We dissolve to what we know by the hazy edges of the frame is a flashback. It is Quinn. It is night time. He is wearing the hood and thick coat we remember from when he stole the car and sat watching Battersby's house. Now he is standing outside Battersby's house. He uses the screwdriver to prise open the back door and enters the house. He looks over to the table where Battersby was sitting earlier, and sees he has gone – presumably to bed. He creeps over to where the sideboard is. The curtains are open and the room is lit only by the street lamp outside. However, just as he has the letter in his hand, he turns and finds Battersby standing behind him, his eyes still bandaged. He has the look of a zombie, his sightless head swivelling, his hands grasping at the air.

Quinn stays still for a moment. Battersby seems to be listening. Now and again his fingers claw out towards things around him like a drowning man feeling for something to save his life. We wonder whether Battersby is sleepwalking. Then Quinn moves quickly towards the door momentarily brushing past Battersby as he does. Battersby reaches out wildly, to grab him, but misses and in his speed he loses his balance and falls on to the display case containing the stuffed wolf. His head crashes through the lid and the glass shatters, leaving jagged sharp edges all around. A dark plume of blood shoots upwards and Battersby's body shudders violently as if he is being electrocuted.

Quinn runs.

Cut to Quinn speaking on the phone in a call box.

Then to blue lights coming towards the house.

Back in the arrivals lounge at Calais it is now empty apart from Quinn standing there holding Katya.

He puts his hand in his pocket and brings out the purple envelope from Battersby's house.

He looks at it for a few moments.

Then he heads off towards the desk.

We see Quinn pointing at the ferry to Dover being loaded up.

Cut to Quinn and Katya walking up the gangplank and on to the boat. Then cut to them standing at the back of the boat watching the bow doors closing.

A high shot of the boat ploughing across the channel away from Calais. The camera tracks down lower towards the ship, zooming closer, then closer, on to the ship's funnels spouting black smoke, then closer still until the black smoke almost fills the screen. The thump thump thump of the engine grows louder in the mix and the camera seems to float down through the smoke and the smoke becomes a little thinner and we see faint, blurred, coloured flowers within the smoke. The flowers resolve into a wallpaper pattern and we follow the thin trail of smoke along the wallpaper to a fireplace. In the hearth a mound of papers, cards, photographs and other ephemera has been set alight and it is beginning to burn furiously. Blackness is eating away the papers like a time-lapse film of mould engulfing a dead animal. The camera tilts to the side to show that a few items have spilled on to the carpet where the fire is also beginning to take. A rapid high-pitched beeping rises on the soundtrack which we recognise as a smoke alarm.

We track away from the burning papers towards the foot of a bed. A pair of naked feet with painted toenails. The camera crawls up a prone body to reveal a woman in a red dressing gown with a leopard-print fur collar. It is Mathilde Pelletier. Motionless, seemingly asleep. A slow panning shot around the room reveals piles of crumpled clothes, crushed packs of cigarettes, an uneaten cake inside a gaping cardboard box, a bowl of cereal with a cigarette stubbed out in it. On the bedside table we see an empty bottle of whisky and a pile of screwed-up pill wrappers. The thump thump thump sound of the ship's engine on the soundtrack changes and we realise that it is someone knocking on Mathilde's door. The knocking gets louder and louder, frantic even. The smoke alarm is shrieking, the fire is crackling, and the room is filling with poisonous fumes, but Mathilde seems oblivious to everything. Then the camera dollies away from Mathilde and pulls back quickly out of the room, as if embarrassed to have disturbed this scene. It somehow melts through the door and we see that the people hammering on it are French police, gendarmes, and we leave the gendarmes knocking on the door and track backwards down an old spiral wooden staircase. We pass an ancient lift in a steel mesh cage moving upwards, with no one in it. We pass an old lady in nightwear putting the rubbish outside her flat. She stares at the camera as if it is a passing ghost. We track backwards down the stairs and out into the light. We are in a French city. The camera rises higher and it is the road that Mathilde has spoken of earlier, Rue Daguerre, in Montparnasse. The tall, dark Montparnasse Tower looms over everything. The knocking sound fades away and the camera rises up high over Paris. We pause for a high shot of the whole city, then we move down again through a series of lap dissolves into the Montparnasse cemetery and the music comes back loudly, a crescendo of dark, dissonant chords. The gates of the cemetery melt into a mid shot of Samuel Beckett's grave, and on the grave, among the scattering of pale yellow leaves, is a purple envelope, like the one Battersby used, in a see-through plastic wrapper.

The camera moves close to show the words *For Quinn* handwritten on it.

Then we hear on the soundtrack a hissing, spluttering sound and there is a slow dissolve to Mathilde's flat again where we see that water is being poured on to the mound of burning papers and that the fire is out.

Over these images a voiceover comes in – it is a lawyer in the courtroom.

'You see, ladies and gentlemen of the jury, this man, the accused, Mr John Ireland, was not involved in Detective Inspector Battersby's sad death at all.'

Close-up on the ashes and remaining scraps of unburned material on the floor.

Letters, papers and photographs, all crumpled and scorched.

'Battersby's death was an accident – admittedly, caused in part by Mr Quinn breaking in.'

The camera tracks to a tangle of cassette tape, disgorged from its plastic case, half melted and blackened by the fire.

'But as we know, Mr Quinn had a very good reason for breaking in. He was there to remove a letter. A letter which he would use to expose this violent and suicidal man and thereby protect Miss Pelletier from harm. The letter I have here in my hand, in fact.'

The camera moves away from the unravelled cassette tape and noses in on one particular semi-incinerated photograph. It is of a couple sitting side by side in a restaurant. They are very close to each other and look happy together. A plate of snails is in front of them and she is holding one in silver tongs and showing the man how to extract the body from the shell.

'In fact the real culprit in this sorry affair might well be that woman, Mathilde Pelletier. If she was here she would also have a lot to answer for. But unfortunately, as we know, Miss Pelletier has disappeared. So all we can deal with today is the issue of Mr Ireland's culpability.'

We recognise the woman in the scorched photograph as Mathilde.

We recognise the man as John Ireland.

If this really was a film, here is where the words THE END would appear on the screen, in wobbly white italics.

But it isn't.

My statement ended with such a climax that I thought that everyone in the courtroom might applaud. It made me think I should have gone to drama school. You might have guessed that not everything in my statement to the court was true. Between you and me, a lot had to be changed. I had to add things, expand things, reduce things, leave things out, and elaborate on certain aspects to take attention away from others. What did that policeman say? Truth is 80 per cent assumption and 20 per cent fact.

Fiona's mum and dad had to be protected. And of course Katya needed to be protected too. And my parents in Cumbria would not have enjoyed hearing the real truth.

After all, when all's said and done, what is real? Who knows what actually happened in any given set of circumstances? Or why? Historians argue about events for years and they never agree. So can there ever be a true version of anything?

I don't remember much now, just blurs of colour, like lights caught in long exposures. All I can say is that Katya and I are safe. And the French police managed to put out the fire, and Mathilde Pelletier was saved. For all you know, she could be with me now, looking over my shoulder as I type.

I believe that no one in this world is innocent. I believe that we are all implicated in everything that happens everywhere. That's the fact of the matter. Everybody's story is both a lie and a truth, all at the same time. We just have to decide which version we like the best.

Acknowledgements

Thanks to my wife, Sarah-Clare Conlon, for her love, advice and support. Thanks, too, to Nicholas Royle; to Luke Brown, Billy Cowan, Nick Thompson and Stephen May; and to Tim Shearer, Zoë McLean and Zena Barrie at Confingo.

Out of the Dark was developed from a short story, 'Insight', which I wrote for the anthology *We Were Strangers: Stories Inspired by Unknown Pleasures* (Confingo Publishing, 2018).